The Kimsara Detective Agency

Dog Gone It

Marty Meyer-Gad

Growth Affirm Press

published by
Growth Affirm Press

Copyright © 2016 by Marty Meyer-Gad

Dedicated to our dogs, especially Aggie and Stasha, whose painful disappearance inspired much of this story. Thanks to my husband, Bruno, and son, Joshua, for sharing these losses.

Thanks to the sixth, seventh and eight grade students I taught or met through extra curricular activities. Your curiosity inspired many of the characters in this series.

Growth Affirming Company
P.O. Box 3582
Mankato, MN 66002

www.growthaffirm.com

The Kimsara Detective Agency: Dog Gone It
Title ID 6070146
ISBN 978-0001380459

The Kimsara Detective Agency

Dog Gone It

I looked out my window at stale snow, glad I would soon escape. Winter had worn out its welcome way before Christmas vacation.

I felt light and bubbly as I bounded down the steps assuring my mother, "I turned in most of my assignments already. What I have left fits in my backpack."

"Are you sure you don't want a ride to school?"

"I'm fine walking to school."

My brother, Justin, dragged a box filled with homework and a fourth grade social studies project toward the door. Mother picked up the box. I gladly held the door open for them, bid them goodbye and bolted upstairs.

I pulled off my jeans and straightened my leggings into the knee-high, heeled boots my mother hated. I yanked my hair from its pony tail scrunchie. A snappy sweater in swirls of blue and purple slipped over my head flowing almost to my boot tops.

As I brushed my hair, I looked at my reflection with pride. As a sixth grader I had moved from being myself to being a somebody. My popularity had risen as I prepared for the mystery trip we would begin tomorrow. My father promised it would be unforgettable. I would be with my father for at least a full month. My father who was seldom home for more than a week at a time, promised to travel with us for a whole month. He hinted we might extend the trip to six months.

Irrepressible joy sprinted me back down the steps. I created my desired image by adding my winter coat, Cossack hat and matching gloves. I grabbed my lunch from the fridge, stuffing it into my backpack.

Yesterday's sun had melted the last of the sidewalk ice allowing me to cover the six-blocks to school in a heartbeat. The slow pace of the morning classes did not drag my spirits down.

I flew out of the classroom when the lunch bell rang, pulled my lunch from my locker and headed to the cafeteria. I had packed everything I needed so I could immediately sit down. I would avoid my daily quandary of where to sit. I was a computer whiz and welcome at the nerds' table even though I abhorred the nerd label. My choir credentials offered me a seat with the musicians. The jocks and artists were entertaining when I joined them. I was friends with everyone. So every day I had a choice.

Today I sat down at an empty table expecting with shaky confidence that cool kids would choose me. Immediately Glo Smith (pronounced with a long i), the most popular girl in our grade, sat next to me. My heart nearly stopped. Glo's friends joined us asking me my family's destination. They were disappointed that I wasn't sure and wouldn't be able to text or email until I got back. As the table cleared Glo and I were alone. I told Glo, in strict confidence, where I thought we were going.

All afternoon kids wished me well and named my destination thanks to their Glo connection. I regretted talking to Glo.

At the end of the day when I stopped by each of my teachers I clarified that I really didn't know my family's final destination. I apologized that my father wouldn't let me keep up with the class through my computer while we were gone. I thanked them for letting me work ahead assuring them they would complete any missed work when I returned.

I hurried home, changed into my jeans, sweatshirt and sneakers before the rest of the family arrived. I busied myself in the kitchen nibbling on vegetables as I put together a salad from everything left in the vegetable crisper.

My mother startled me with, "Hi, Sara. Is that your snack or our dinner?"

"Hi, Mom. There's not enough for dinner. What **are** we having for dinner? The refrigerator is bare."

My father walked in adding, "As it should be considering we'll be leaving tomorrow."

The front door slammed and Justin announced for all to hear, "I'm home and ready to go."

"Good idea," Father responded

Justin lit up. "You mean we can leave for the trip now?"

"No, Silly," I corrected while handing him the last carrot.

Our father explained, "We're going out to eat. When we get back we can finish packing before bed."

Chapter Two

By eight o'clock that evening all the suitcases and backpacks were lined up by the back door. Knowing putting a lit sparkler into an envelope would have been easier than tucking me and my brother in bed, Mother showed videos of our past vacations while playing soft, soothing background music. Chatter over the videos decreased with time. By nine-thirty everyone was ready for bed.

I woke up disappointed that the clock glowed 1:00 A.M.. I lay in bed watching time crawl. At 4:00 A.M. I gave up on sleeping and got dressed. Tiptoeing downstairs I heard whispers from the kitchen where the rest of the family was already dressed and eating breakfast.

I joined them. While buttering my favorite, a blueberry muffin, I asked, "Will we take the extra muffins with us?"

"No," my mother replied. "We'll throw them in the freezer with the bread. George, I think we're a little ahead of schedule."

"We are very early. What should we do?" he pondered.

I proposed, "Listen to you tell us about where we are going and what we will be doing."

"Hmm, interesting idea, but I told you that will wait until we are all in our seats on the plane. I suggest we

4

leave for the airport early. Kids double check your rooms. Make sure you have everything and let's meet in the car."

Justin and I raced each other upstairs, ran through our rooms and back down. We grabbed our backpacks and shot out the door into the morning darkness. Justin heaved open the driver's side of the rental car, zipped across the back seat and locked the door just as I reached to open it. I huffed around to the inferior position behind, not across, from the driver. My glare turned seraphic as our parents appeared with the last of our carry on luggage.

"Ready for an adventure?" my father asked with a proud twinkle in his voice.

"Yes, Sir," Justin snapped while grabbing the hat I had hidden behind my back.

Under my breath I growled, "Give me back Natasha."

"Secure your seat belts," Father commanded as he pulled out of our driveway.

I ignored the Christmas displays we were passing, trying to quietly get my hat back.

Justin held it next to the koala bear attached to his backpack. "Dad, Sara's hat is the same color as the kangaroo fur of my koala bear. So it's made of kangaroo fur too, isn't it?"

"No, give Natasha back to your sister."

I flinched. Having a hat with a name seemed so infantile. I treasured that my father knew I had named it. Two years ago I wanted a pet so bad and had been lobbying for one in every possible way. My father couldn't soften my mother's no pet policy. So when he had returned from a trip with a furry hat he wasn't surprised I considered it my pet and named it.

He continued, "Sara's Russian style hat would look silly in short kangaroo fur." Noticing Justin returning my hat he complimented, "Sara, you look good in that hat."

"Thanks, Dad," I beamed while putting it on.

Mother looked up from her new smart phone. "Sara, I thought we agreed you weren't bringing that hat. You won't be needing it on the trip. We've had so little snow and cold you don't even need it now."

I winced.

5

Gratefully my mother changed the subject. "George, there are some thin bands of snow between here and the airport."

"Are you getting the hang of the new phone, Dear?"

"I still don't see why I couldn't bring my own phone instead of this temporary international one," Mother snapped.

As we approached I 94 Justin exclaimed, "Snow angels," as huge flakes tumbled across the windshield.

Father asked Mother, "Nancy, does 94 or 694 look better?"

"Traffic is starting to slow on both. An accident on 94 makes 694 a better bet. Is the road getting slick?"

"A little, but visibility is the problem. I'll exit on Bass Lake Road. We'll find a coffee shop and wait until the snow clears a little. We've got plenty of time."

As we exited the freeway, Justin screamed. I looked at my wide-eyed brother and beyond him at the car speeding into us. Before I could scream the car jolted. Everyone was slapped to the left as metal clashed with metal. Then everything thing went black. I saw a piercing white light. As my eyes acclimated I saw my parents and brother. The light faded and I fell into a coma.

Chapter Three

I spent most of January hospitalized in a coma. When it lifted, physical therapy slowly restored my muscle tone. Meetings with Dr. Philomena Hughes were standoffs. Prod as the doctor did, I refused to discuss the death of my parents and brother. Talking wouldn't bring them back, so why bother?

The day my medical doctor released me from the hospital, I didn't hear a word he said. I just smiled and nodded. My Aunt Patty took notes. When my Uncle Art went to get the car, I balked as a wheelchair approached. I had spent time in physical therapy and felt I could walk, my legs were strong again.

Stepping into the chilly hall, I looked in the direction of the intensive care unit. I had spent time there. Had my parents really been with me after they died? Was it a dream? Part of me wanted to stay, not leave them. I had no sense of their presence once I woke from the coma. They had promised my life would be better. How could they know that? They had left me behind. I felt empty and alone.

Then I felt guilty because I wasn't alone. I had new parents: my Aunt Patty and Uncle Art. Their son, my cousin, Jerry, was he now my brother? Weird to go home to strangers, people you knew and had celebrated family holidays with. But, did I really know them?

7

As I walked back to the room, I stumbled and knew arguing against the wheelchair was premature. So I sat down in it as the doctor shook Aunt Patty's hand and then mine, wishing me a full recovery.

The trip home was filled with animated chatter between Aunt Patty and Uncle Art. I managed appropriate grunts now and then in accord with the cadence, not content of the conversation. I smiled and remembered they had a dog, Jerry's dog.

Aunt Patty explained, "We didn't change much of Jerry's room for you."

"Patty thought of bringing over your bedding, but decided against it in case you wanted to redecorate." Uncle Art added, "Jerry repainted the room and took down his posters."

I surprised them with, "Right, Jerry brought paint samples to the hospital and told me to pick the color. When I told him I didn't care, he threatened he would paint the walls black and blue. His girlfriend, Peaches, suggested a soft lavender. Is that the color he painted it?"

"Yes, they did it in stripes of flat and semigloss lavender," confirmed Aunt Patty. "The room looks elegant."

A few miles later, I confessed. "I forgot you live in the country." I pointed to five animals in the field not too far from the highway. "Are those buffalo?"

"Yes, though technically they are bison. There are several herds near us," Uncle Art explained. That gave me an idea. He added, "Sara, I see that twinkle in your eye. No, you can't have a pet bison or buffalo."

"Uncle Art you told Jerry you wanted a daughter more than a buffalo when he asked for one. Now you have a daughter so Jerry suggested I try for a buffalo." To clear the silence that hung heavy in the car, I continued, "I'm kidding. I like buffalo from a distance."

I overheard my aunt quietly say, "Art, she's talking, holding an actual conversation."

He sighed, "Relax. It'll work out."

Chapter Four

Ten minutes later I wondered, "Did Jerry take his dog with him to college?"

"No, pets aren't allowed in his dorm," Aunt Patty clarified. "Mitzy will probably adopt you."

We exited the freeway, continuing on county roads.

"Is that the Whistlestop High School?" I inquired as we passed a complex of brick buildings.

"Yes, and more." Uncle Art explained, "The high school, the junior high and the elementary school are all interconnected."

"Will I be going there?"

"That's one of the things we'll discuss with Dr. Hughes tomorrow." Then Aunt Patty looked at a text on her phone noting, "Jerry says he is home and has dinner ready for us. Sara, do you like Chinese?"

"Yes," I declared as we turned down the country road leading to my new home. I saw more horses than cows, more fields than houses and more patches of brown than snow. I had been at Uncle Art and Aunt Patty's house several times. Most recently I accompanied my mother when she dropped off her computer, tablet and phone before the trip in. Her sister could then send them to her if necessary.

As we pulled in the driveway Uncle Art announced, "Sara, welcome to your new home."

I didn't want a new home. I got out of the car trying to muster enough energy to look happy.

As Uncle Art opened the house door, Mitzy ran out and up to me. I bent down to pet her. Peaches had slipped into Jerry's boots, grabbed his coat and ran out to welcome us. As we embraced, I sobbed uncontrollably. After a few minutes, Mitzy barked as Jerry appeared in the doorway announcing, "Dinner, and you, dear women, are getting cold."

I reached into my coat and pulled out one of the tissues. I blew my nose and dried my eyes as we walked into the house.

Upon seeing us Jerry announced with glee, "Yeah, Sara's crying." His parents stood in shocked silence.

I threw off my coat and tried to punch him. He wove to avoid the punches trying to tickle me between my thrusts. Mitzy tried separating us, tripping both of us. Once on the floor Mitzy licked my face until I laughed. Jerry stood, then reached down and pulled me to my feet. He put his arm around me and escorted me to the table.

As we sat down Aunt Patty demanded, "What was that?"

"Sibling affection," replied Peaches.

After blessing the food Jerry announced the menu.

"All my favorites. How did you know?"

"I'm clairvoyant when it comes to my sister," bragged Jerry.

Peaches stared him down until he revealed, "I checked your mom's phone. She had a standing order for Chinese so that's what I got. It might taste a little different because it's from the Whistlestop Chinese instead of the place she used."

I enjoyed the familiar food but was uncomfortable when Jerry explained his relief seeing me cry. "Sara, you've got to understand. It's okay to cry."

When I teared up he added, "Crying helps with the healing."

Peaches added, "You told us in the hospital that you were afraid to cry because you weren't sure you could stop. You proved today you could stop."

"You don't have to hide your tears from us," Uncle Art assured me.

Chapter Five

After dinner Jerry and Peaches took me to my room. The dresser contained my clothes. I wondered what happened to the clothes I had packed for the trip. Most of them were summer clothes.

Before I could ask about them I saw my mother's computer sitting on the desk next to her cell phone and tablet. "That isn't my computer," I explained as Aunt Patty walked into the room.

"Was yours better than this one?" Aunt Patty questioned.

"Definitely not," I admitted.

"Any problem using this one instead?"

"No, this is a great upgrade."

"Are you going to have a problem with her passwords?" cautioned Peaches.

"I doubt it," Jerry claimed as he pointed to post-its with passwords attached to the side of the computer.

"Your mother would want you to use her phone and tablet too," Aunt Patty decided.

"Time for us to scoot," Jerry announced. "Now if you have any problems with our parents, don't hesitate to call me. Both Peaches and my numbers are on the phone."

"Thanks for all the time the two of you spent with me at the hospital," I acknowledged while hugging them good bye.

Once they had gone I said good night. I urged my tired body upstairs. I cried myself to sleep with tears of relief. I was home.

11

The next day after much discussion among Aunt Patty, Uncle Art, Jerry, Peaches and Dr. Hughes; I agreed to return to school in Elk River in a week or two. I wanted to be steady enough not to need a wheelchair or walker. I hoped words wouldn't keep eluding me. The blanks that masked my thoughts angered me.

Before ending the session Dr. Hughes queried, "Have you been in contact with any of your classmates?"

"No, I told everyone I would be out of the country and wouldn't be answering emails or texts while I was gone. My father forbad us to use Facebook. Why?"

"I contacted your school about your return. They thought you had died in the accident and had a memorial service for you at school."

My eyes widened. "Does that mean I can skip school?"

"No," boomed from all directions.

"The school is making an announcement correcting the error."

"Now don't let anyone call you Lazarus," Jerry insisted.

"Seriously," Dr. Hughes continued, "you might want to contact your friends before going back."

"I have everyone's phone number and email address on my computer. Without it, I can't," I pouted with relief.

"I'll get your email account and address book through your mom's computer when we get home," Uncle Art promised. He accomplished that task within a half hour of us returning home.

That evening I called a friend but hung up when my first word evaporated. Aunt Patty witnessed my frustration. She must have contacted the extended family because all of a sudden, day and night I got calls from cousins, aunts and even uncles. If I didn't respond to a text message, I could expect a call on the house landline. Each day I got more comfortable finding words. I got the courage to email a few friends but due to a computer glitch I didn't get their responses.

The two weeks passed too quickly. For the first time in my life, I dreaded going to school.

12

Chapter Six

When Dr. Hughes called the principal about my return, she suggested I return on the next Monday. Since it was an inservice day no students would be present. All of my teachers would be able to meet with me after lunch.

That Monday Aunt Patty, Dr. Hughes and I met at the coffee shop near the school. Peaches joined us. I wore sad clothes: old jeans, a black hoodie, old boots and my winter jacket. After we ordered our food, Dr. Hughes began, "Sara, what do your clothes say?"

"What?" I had no idea what she meant.

"I know you hate being asked how you feel. So I am wondering if you chose those clothes for a special reason."

"I just got dressed." I looked at what I was wearing. "They're clean clothes. Was I supposed to dress up?" I muttered defensively.

"No, is this what you would have worn to school before the accident?"

I blushed. Everyone ate in silence for a few minutes before I admitted, "I never would have worn this to school. These are my after school clothes."

"They are fine for your meeting with the teachers today," Dr. Hughes assured me. "Have you decided what you will be wearing tomorrow?"

"No," I confessed. I did not look forward to going back to school.

13

"May I suggest you wear clothes that make you feel confident, even if that's not how you feel? You said you don't want the kids to pity you. So don't wear pitiable clothes."

"It's my fault," claimed Aunt Patty. She looked at me as she continued, "I thought about encouraging you to change your clothes."

"However, you are uncomfortable telling your new daughter what to do," suggested Dr. Hughes. Aunt Patty blushed.

Then she quizzed me, "Sara, if your mother, Patty, had told you to change into different clothes, what would you have done?"

"Changed, probably into the outfit I worn for Church on Sunday."

"Would you have been mad about being told to change?"

"No," I paused and thought for a moment. "Yes, maybe a little. Today I didn't care what I wore. That's not true. I really don't want to go back to school."

"Sara!" Aunt Patty exclaimed in surprise.

Dr. Hughes put her hand over Aunt Patty's. "Tell your mother more precisely what you are thinking."

"I know I have to go back to school, but I'm scared."

"That's an honest statement that your teachers need to hear." Looking at her watch she added, "Oh, how time has flown. We need to leave now. Your teachers are waiting for us."

Aunt Patty paid the bill and we walked the block to school.

Chapter Seven

The principal met us at the door. "Welcome back, Sara. The sixth grade teachers are all in the media center waiting for you."

I sighed and would have slowed down if my homeroom teacher, Mrs. Gervase, didn't appear as we turned the corner. After a welcoming embrace, she gathered me around my waist and escorted me into the media center. The teachers all approached welcoming me.

I felt overwhelmed and teary eyed from the attention. The librarian, Mr. Parks, whistled and on cue, Taurus, the library dog appeared. Assessing the situation the dog immediately nuzzled into my folded arms, making me laugh. He pushed me into one of the chairs forming a circle. When I sat, the big lab mix rested his head in my lap. As I petted him I relaxed.

The principal began, "Sara, we are so sorry for the loss of your family. We are committed to do everything we can to help you in your return to school.

"Over the next week or so each teacher will help you catch up with what you have missed. We don't want you to try to do everything at once."

Mrs. Gervase added. "We've recruited some companions who will be sitting next to you and helping you catch up."

Dr. Hughes then addressed the group as she passed out her business cards. "I am available to help. It may take Sara a little while to get her mind fully functioning at her pre-accident level. She has agreed to help out a psychology student who is researching the effects of a coma. This student, Ms. Paige Georgia, will accompany her during her first week back at school and may be visiting once a week or so after that. She will present a packet to each teacher tomorrow outlining ways you can get involved with her project if you wish. You do not need to do anything but allow her in your classroom.

Peaches stood up and scanned the room before speaking. "On behalf of Sara and her family I thank you for your warm welcome and for all the help you will be giving her in the future."

Then she looked at me expectantly, "Sara, is there anything you wish to say?" Dr. Hughes had prepared me the last time we met for possible things I might want to say.

I looked up then addressed the dog in my lap. "I'm scared. I get embarrassed because sometimes I can't help crying. Sometimes I can't think of the words I want to say."

The teachers offered a flurry of support and understanding.

Aunt Patty sounded proud as she told me, "You're getting better every day." She then addressed the teachers, "Please let us know if there is anything we can do to help Sara with her school work."

After an awkward silence, Aunt Patty stood and walked toward me. "Thanks for giving us this time to meet with you. I think it's time for us to head home."

As we prepared to leave Mr. Parks invited me to visit Taurus in the media center anytime I wanted.

Chapter Eight

On the way home Aunt Patty and I discussed clothes. I decided I would wear the same outfit I had worn on my last day of school.

When I mentioned that none of my friends had returned my emails, She reminded me to check the spam and trash folders. When I did, I found every one of them had been answered and people were looking forward to my return. I went to bed feeling reconnected with my classmates. I awoke with cautious anticipation.

Peaches arrived early to drive me to school. When I saw her she commented, "You look great in that outfit."

"Thanks. I didn't know your last name was Georgia."

"That's why people call me Peaches. My legal name is Paige Amelia Georgia. Ready to go?" she asked loud enough for Aunt Patty to hear.

Aunt Patty came into the kitchen. "Sara, have a good day at school." Then looking at the two of us, she inquired, "Did you coordinate on your outfits?"

"No, Mrs. C., this blue suit is my job interview outfit, the totality of my professional wardrobe. I must admit it does go well with Sara's."

"It does. Thanks for taking her to school. I hope you'll stay for supper."

"That's the plan," Peaches acknowledged as we left.

In the car Peaches summarized what we had discussed for hours over the past couple of weeks. Then she started quizzing me. "What do you expect to happen when you get to school?"

"Anything and everything. Some people will think I'm new to the school. Some might be uncomfortable around me."

"Why?"

"For any reason. They don't like what I'm wearing, or are thinking about my parents dying, or what I said last December."

"Is that your problem?"

I hesitated. This was a new question. "No, what other people think or feel is not my problem. But, I don't think I should try to make them uncomfortable." After an extended silence I added, "Unless they deserve it."

Peaches cautioned, "Revenge doesn't suit you, Sara." We had arrived at the school. Peaches asked about the source of my comment. I had gained a strange bubble of confidence during our ride. I ignored the question quickly exiting the car and heading toward school while Peaches parked the car.

I walked into the school toward my locker as the first buses were unloading. All of a sudden a voice boomed from behind me, "Sara, is that that you? You're back."

I turned into the shocking embrace of Glo Smith. She released me while gushing, "How was Australia?" Those around Glo gasped audibly.

I wanted to laugh, scream, say something mean in the awkward silence.

Glo explained to those around her, "She told me where she was going, that's why I know. So how was it, Sara?"

I calmly stated, "I didn't go to Australia." I returned to settling things in my locker feeling pity for Glo.

Becky Jones, a special needs student who had the locker next to me turned, addressing Glo, "She didn't go anywhere, Glo. She was in an accident that killed her parents and brother. She was in a coma. Didn't you listen to yesterday's announcements?"

"Thanks, Becky," I whispered while a swarm of students smothered me in apologies.

A red-faced Glo walked away from the lockers as Peaches entered the school. I walked toward homeroom with several students who started sharing jokes and making everyone laugh. The incident gave me confidence to face the day.

By lunch time I was exhausted. Peaches approached me offering, "Nap or lunch what's first?"

"Nap," I admitted though was not looking forward to the cot in the nurse's office. Peaches surprised me by escorting me to the futon at the back of the media center. A newly cased pillow beckoned. I slipped out of my boots and spread out as Peaches covered me with the fleece blanket she pulled from her briefcase. Taurus appeared from nowhere, snuggling beside me as I melted into sleep.

Chapter Nine

Two hours later I woke up as Taurus tugged on my pillow. I looked at my watch and immediately popped up. I had missed lunch, math class and was late for social studies. As I rebooted, Taurus left returning with Peaches.

In panic I spouted, "I'm late...I missed...oh, no...."

"Are you hungry?" Peaches calmly asked.

"Yes, but..."

"Then lunch is next. I'm surprised you made it through the whole morning. After you eat, you can go to class. You were supposed to skip your last period for that last physical therapy session, remember?"

I nodded.

"When I saw you were sleeping so soundly I called your Aunt Patty. She rearranged things. You'll stay for your last period today. Tomorrow you'll come for homeroom. Then I'll take you for physical therapy and you'll come back for the classes you missed today."

"I could skip physical therapy."

"Not an option. The plan is to gradually reintegrate you into school."

"But, I'm behind." I wondered if I would ever catch up.

"So?" Peaches paused while we both ate. As we finished Peaches explained, "Sara, you are not behind. You are where you are. You are alive and healing. None of your teachers seem concerned about your catching up.

20

They'll all work with you. You do what you can and relax. Have some fun while you're catching up."

Easy for you to say was my unspoken thought. Then I smiled thinking back to my morning meeting with Glo. I remembered that in each of the classes I did attend some student had been assigned as my assistant. They whispered the backstory when I felt left out, helped me get situated in ongoing projects and kept my mind from wandering. That assistance continued for several months. While the fog started lifting, I wasn't myself. As I needed less help with school work I realized part of me was missing, or at least it felt that way. As I tolerated the full school day, Peaches withdrew as my driver. Aunt Patty or Uncle Art got me to and from school. They were going out of their way for me so my life could get back to normal. In gratitude I used a lot of energy to act normal, to act happy.

On one rare occasion Jerry had been recruited to pick me up. As I hopped in his car he announced, "I wish I had more time. We could celebrate the first seventy degree day with a picnic in the park."

"I'm just glad you could pick me up so Mom and Dad could both go to their meetings."

"Mitzy's going to want to go for a walk when she sees me. Poor thing, I won't have time for that."

I heard him as I drifted near sleep. Groggily I sputtered, "I could take her for a walk. That's the least I could do."

"You're too tired. Instead of a walk you could go in the woods, find a comfortable spot to sit and toss sticks for her to fetch. She'll get exercise and you'll both enjoy the sunshine."

After he left, I changed my clothes and did just that. After a few tosses, Mitzi ran off. I sat down on one of many freshly cut stumps, leaning against a tree. I was falling asleep when she returned followed by what? a larger dog? As it got closer I knew it was a black bear. My mind processed the reality. The bland feeling I had since the death of my parents and brother repressed any fear. So what if the bear killed me? At times I felt dead already.

The bear was my totem animal. I had been told that years before when I visited a reservation with my father.

The woman explained I could trust a bear if it looked me in the eyes before it approached.

The bear's eyes registered understanding like my mother's could. When Mitzy laid down at my feet the bear followed. I slipped down next to the bear resting my head in its fur. In my heart of hearts I heard a summons to let go of my pain. Bury it deep. Bury it in the bear. I relaxed into sleep feeling sorrow draining from me into the bear at the same time peace flowed from Mitzy's paw which now rested on my leg. I woke when the bear moved. Mitzy barked. The bear slowly retreated. I brushed myself off. When I stood Mitzy ran to my side. I instinctively leashed her and we approached the house as my new mom, Aunt Patty, drove up. I acted like I was coming back from a walk with the dog.

I told no one about the bear I occasionally hung out with, the bear where I buried my sorrows.

ChapterTen

By May I had caught up with my school work. I felt in control of my body and my mind. I met less frequently with Dr. Hughes. As I honestly responded to questions I realized that while I was friendly with everyone at school, I had no friends. I used to have friends, girls I would do things with, call every night. Then last year my two dearest friends moved to other states. My parents objected to my having a cell phone. So when my classmates got them I was left out. I didn't hang out after school even though I lived within walking distance from the middle school. I had to get home to open the door for my brother when he got off the bus from elementary school. My mother couldn't guarantee she would be home from work in time. My father in ways discouraged me from making friends. He traveled a lot and wanted my full attention when he came home.

Then Dr. Hughes challenged me. "What can you do to make friends?"

I answered, "Change schools. Elk River is too far from home. When I went back, I was ..."

"Fragile?"

"Yeah, I was fragile and some people still treat me like I am. I don't feel normal around them." I preempted the expected comment with, "I know that's my feeling, not necessarily reality. I think if I go to Whistlestop for school I can start over and as the new kid make friends that live close enough to get together."

23

"Would you want to change schools now?"

"No, in September. I am already signed up for the Whistlestop seventh grade summer camping trip. Aunt Patty, thinks it will be a great opportunity to meet some of my classmates ahead of time."

Dr. Hughes seemed satisfied with my progress. Our meetings were less frequent and would have ended if my Father hadn't been such a man of mystery. We agreed to break for the summer and meet again at least once after I settled in my new school.

Once the decision had been made to change schools, I freely shared the news, giving me a new wave of popularity. Since I now had my mom's cell phone I stayed connected but found that I didn't really enjoy some who sought me out. Fortunately the month passed quickly. I parted from the school and a past life without regrets.

At home Aunt Patty began gardening with a contagious enthusiasm that drew me in. A few plants were poking through the ground when I left for camp.

Two weeks later sunburned, pocked with mosquito bites, deliriously happy, I exited the camp bus. Aunt Patty was waiting. She walked up and embraced me.

"Looks like camp agreed with you," she laughed as we waited for our camping gear to be unloaded.

"It did, Aunt Patty," I beamed as I pulled my new friend to my side. "This is Kim. She lives near us. Could we give her a ride home?"

"Sure."

"You're Jerry's Mom, Mrs. C. aren't you?"

"Yes, and how do you know Jerry?"

"He hangs out with my brothers sometimes. We live right next door to you. We're the Porters. I was supposed to call my mom when we got in. She works in town and would come and pick me up. But if you could take me home..."

"We'll take you home," my aunt agreed as she handed Kim her phone. "Call your mom and tell her that."

"Thanks Mrs. C." After a few minutes on the phone Kim handed the phone back. "My mom wants to talk to you."

While my aunt and Kim's mother talked we loaded our things into the car. We were deep in conversation when my aunt joined us. "Kim, we'll take you home. Your mom said she'll be home at the usual time."

"Thanks, Mrs. C."

"No problem. Sara, I'm so glad you made a friend who lives near us."

Chapter Eleven

That evening at supper I gushed through camp stories. Then I remembered girls talking about financial concerns. I had questioned whether I was a financial burden to my new parents. So I asked, "How much does it cost for me to be on your cell phone plan?"

I wondered if I saw guilt or embarrassment as Uncle Art and Aunt Patty looked at each other.

Uncle Art finally spoke. "You're not on our plan. I'm not sure how much your plan costs. I probably should investigate that."

"If you're not paying for my phone, who is?"

"We should have had this conversation sooner," Aunt Patty confessed. "In a way your father is paying the phone bill." I glanced at Uncle Art prompting Aunt Patty to add, "Your birthfather."

Before I could verbalize my shock, Uncle Art continued. "Your father set up a trust in case anything happened to him. This trust had been set up through his company by his accountant."

"Wasn't my father self-employed?"

"Yes, and no. I am not sure I understand it all. After your father died, a man identifying himself as your father's business partner contacted me. He gave me a legal copy of your father's will. It declared us the legal guardians of any dependents if both he and his wife died. We knew about that because he had us sign such an agreement before you were born.

"All of his assets were to go in a trust for his dependents until they reached twenty-one. Then it listed some expenses that the trust would pay out until then. Cell phone was one of the listed expenses. Transportation to and from school was another."

Aunt Patty continued, "When he found out you would be going to Elk River for school he wanted to hire a car service to take you to and from school. We objected. He offered to pay for our mileage to get you to and from school. He even sent us forms to fill out for reimbursement."

"I never sent them in. Did you, Patty?" Uncle Art questioned. "I have been meaning to ask."

"No, I never did. Why?"

"We got a mileage check for February and March in the mail today."

"What did you do with it?" wondered Aunt Patty.

Art reached over to the counter and pulled it out of the stack of mail. "Sara, when we started to get monthly support payments from your trust manager we put them in an account in your name, except for your allowance which we give you. I planned to deposit the mileage check in that account."

I thought back, "That's what you meant when I told you I didn't need an allowance. You said that my father arranged it and the money came from him."

"Yes, but you were still in shock and I didn't know how much to tell you."

I smiled. "Thanks, Uncle Art, I mean, Dad, for acknowledging I am no longer in shock. I am getting back to normal."

As we continued eating I thought. Finally I suggested, "Please don't put that check in my account. I have been feeling guilty about the time and money you have spent getting me to and from school and my appointments. I would feel better if you kept it."

"She has a point. After all, Art, we have been reimbursing Jerry and Peaches when they drive Sara. We could put the money in a new account, the car replacement account we've been talking about for decades."

"I'd like that," I sighed with relief at not being a financial burden and with grateful love for my father. "Can I go over to Kim's after dishes?"

"No!" Uncle Art declared firmly trying to look cross, confounding me. "I'll get the dishes. You can go now."

I got up and hugged him. Then I threw out one of my camp acquired phrases while slapping the back of my hand to my forehead, "Such a drama queen." Before I closed the door, I added a heart-filled, "Thanks, Dad," addressing both my fathers.

Chapter Twelve

Aunt Patty got up early that Saturday morning. She had a writing exercise to complete before she met with her writers' group.

She barely noticed me when I came down and ate breakfast. I grabbed Misty's leash for a walk. I thought I heard a dog barking outside a moment before Misty erupted with counter barks. I opened the door and screamed.

I stood in the open door. Hearing my name and feeling a maternal embrace broke my fixation on the bloody glove at my feet. As the dog-less leash in my hand slipped, Mitzy zipped past me to join the other dog.

I voiced, "The dog...," to the woman holding me. Barking redirected our gaze. I broke free of the embrace and ran, instinctively pulling out my phone.

Aunt Patty's, "Call 9-1-1," made me stop. I dialed the number and handed the phone to her as she passed me running toward the dogs and something on the ground at the edge of the woods, just beyond a patch of prairie grass.

Meanwhile a quick flashback triggered in my brain and my legs became concrete. My analytical mind confirmed I wasn't seeing double. The two dogs looked alike but the family dog, Mitzy, had a pink collar. The other had a brown one. What was on the ground? Was it blood? Is that what was on the dog at the door? I felt faint.

Mitzy ran to me. As I reached down to pet her, my legs weakened and I eased to the ground. I nuzzled into her fur, allowing canine licks and the beginning drizzle to revive me. I refused to retreat into oblivion again. I stood and ran with Mitzy toward my aunt as she said, "Yes, that's our address."

"I'm not sure," my aunt continued into the phone. "I'm trying to get closer."

As I reached her, she handed me the phone which I put to my ear. The growling increased as she inched toward the bloody hunter on the ground.

"That's the dog guarding the body keeping my um...mom from getting closer," I explained to the phone. Meanwhile Mitzy slipped between my aunt and the other dog. Aunt Patty's soft patter quieted the stray dog, whose collar identified him as, "Max."

Mitzy followed Aunt Patty's hand signals to play dead. This created enough distraction for me to hand back the phone and leash the stray dog.

Hearing a groan from the body Mom immediately yelled into the phone, "He's alive."

Max flew into the air when he felt the leash. I steeled my grip with both hands and for the first time took a good look at the bloodied body. Rage erupted in me cementing my hands to the leash. Like a bucking bronco Max demanded to be off the leash, bolting away from the body. He pulled the retractable leash to its full 20 foot length.

As Mom reached down to the body, Max shot to her side, teeth bared. I tried unsuccessfully to hold him back. As he lunged to bite, our dog, our docile, totally non-dominant dog, attacked Max allowing me to control him. The rage within me grew, giving me the strength to pull him from the area.

"Sara, please kennel the dogs," Mom directed. "An ambulance is on its way."

She gave Mitzy the hand signal to kennel up as I pulled the reluctant Max toward the house. His resistance lessened as Mitzy moved beside him.

I started toward the unoccupied sheep pasture but remembered stories of dogs and goats easily getting out of it. I changed course. Mitzy went past her dog house and plopped on the porch step next to the bloody glove. I chained Max to Mitzy's dog house.

Chapter Thirteen

Both dogs howled at distance sirens. Their intensity increased as a police car entered the drive from the south and an ambulance from the north. I stood covering my ears momentarily before pointing to the injured man. Both vehicles stopped inches away from him. An officer got out. As Mom approached her, Mitzy dashed protectively to her side. The officer instantaneously pulled a gun and aimed for our dog.

"No," Mom yelled pushing the officer's arm as her gun discharged, sending the bullet into the siding and her gun to the ground.

"Why are you shooting my dog?" she demanded as the officer picked up her gun.

"We got a report about an uncontrollable dog with the victim. I didn't want it causing problems."

"That dog is now under control," she snapped with distain, pointing to the dog house. "You can put your gun away. I'm putting my dog in the house." Both dogs were in a barking frenzy: Mitzy plastered to Mom's side; Max jumping, straining at the chain linking him to the dog house.

The officer turned to Max, hand on her recently holstered gun.

"Don't you dare shoot that dog either." Mom walked over to Max. With nothing to lose, she shouted with authority, "Max, shut up," while threatening him with a piece of rebar she had pulled out of a flower bed as she passed it. He did, lowering his voice to a whimper. Mitzy had stopped barking and approached as if to comfort him.

I stood by the dog house dazed, watching the EMTs.

The officer walked towards the woods as the EMTs lifted the body to the gurney and continued stabilizing him. After consulting the EMTs the officer walked back toward the house, stating, "I'll take his dog into custody."

"No, you will not," Mom stated.

Seeing the officer's shocked expression, I questioned our legal right to keep the dog. I knew the police took dogs to the township pound, a place she despised.

Mom declared, "The dog has endured enough trauma and doesn't need more in the dog pound. For all we know it could be one of the neighbor's dogs. If it is his dog, tell the family they can pick him up here."

"Are you sure it's a dog and not a wolf?" the officer demanded.

"Wolves don't wear collars," I fabricated. Both dogs stood alert, but quiet. Both looked like wolves, litter mates even. Our chow-husky mix could have posed as a twin for the wolf on the cover of the Alaska magazine sitting on the coffee table.

"I need to take him in case he's responsible for some of the injuries," the officer insisted.

"When that's determined, you know where to find him," Mom countered.

The officer approached the dogs, stopped by insistent growls and barking. Both dogs looked ready to pounce.

"Are you sure you want to take the dog?" Mom needled.

The officer reassessed the situation. As she stared, both dogs growled. "Okay. For now, you keep it here."

Chapter Fourteen

A Whistlestop police car arrived and parked by the pole barn leaving plenty of room for the ambulance to escape. "That's my backup, Jack Lewis, the first officer explained." The two consulted and both headed into the woods.

Taking the leash from me, Mom attached it to Max's collar while removing the chain. We walked both dogs into the house. Mitzy immediately headed to the water bucket, moving aside when unleashed Max approached. After Max drank his share he emptied Mitzy's food dish. Then he joined Mitzy asleep on the dog mat under the living room table.

Mom and I went back outside as the gurney was put into the ambulance. The first officer approached and finally introduced herself as Officer Sally Minks. Then showing us a picture on her cellphone she asked, "Do you know who this man is? He doesn't seem to speak English."

"No. His features are like Jimmy's, who owns the property south of us. But, it's not Jimmy."

"Do you have Jimmy's phone number?"

"Yes, in the house."

"I'll get it," I offered and ran to the house, grateful for the absence of barking as I approached. I checked the dogs. Both were sound asleep.

The ambulance screeched by, sirens blaring as it approached the quiet rural road. The dogs sprang to life. As the siren faded their barks crescendoed.

My, "It's okay," was lost. I demanded, "Mitzy, quiet!" Our dog complied. Then I picked up a wooden spoon locked it in attack mode like my mom had done. Hoping for a repeat performance, I yelled, "Max, shut up!" Silence.

"You stay," I commanded with voice and hand signal. "No barking." Throwing them rawhide chews, I pulled out our looseleaf phonebook opening it to the "N" page figuring like my mom her sister would have filed him under "Neighbor."

Once outside I handed Mom the open phone book. Glancing down the page she found Jimmy's number and dialed it. The female officer approached as Jimmy's phone rang. Her face registered impatience as she listened to the one sided conversation.

"Jimmy, this is Patty Cowley, your neighbor to the north of your property."

"Yes, the one in Sherburne County."

"Were you expecting anyone hunting on your property today?"

"A man was just taken to the hospital."

"I don't know."

"I can't but the police probably could. I'll hang up and have them call you with a picture. Bye."

The restless officer using the open phone book, had dialed Jimmy's number. She counted to ten out loud and pressed send. "Jimmy, I'm Officer Sally Minks with the Sherburne County police department. Can I send you a picture to see if you can identify the man?" As they negotiated, Mom and I headed to the woods, now marked with crime scene ribbon.

"Don't come any closer," Officer Lewis ordered. "Is this your property?"

"Yes," Mom confirmed.

"How far does it go to the south?"

"Just before that tree you've marked with the yellow tape. That's where Jimmy's begins."

"How far back?"

"About seven hundred feet. The marker's hard to see."

He dismissed us with, "That's all."

34

Chapter Fifteen

"Don't you want to know what's out of place?" Mom urged, her hand spanning from the chicken coop to the woods.

"Detective Cory Watkins will be asking that. He should be here within the hour. I'll take the dog," he barked with authority.

"No, like I told the other officer, the dog is staying here," she stated while trying to catch up with his determined stride. I slowly walked away from the crime scene tape.

Officer Minks after ending her phone conversation used the siren to contact her backup. So when we reached the house both dogs were barking.

Over the din Mom acknowledged, "I do have something you or the detective can have." She opened the door slightly, pushing the dogs back. Seeing a foot on the threshold, she turned. "Please wait outside."

I pushed in front of the officer making him move back as I went in. Even though the rain intensified, our rights trumped our hospitality. I watched enough TV to know he couldn't come in without a warrant.

One loud, "Quiet," was successful. I directed the dogs to the kitchen and shut the door to the mud room. I returned to my mom's side.

35

She grabbed a rag while opening the outside door. "This, you can have, or the detective or whoever wants it. It's yours. I don't want it back."

The officer took the piece of old flannel sheet with its weak blood stains. He also picked up the bloody glove from the step.

Officer Minks approached, popping open the umbrella she had pulled from her vehicle. She looked at the stained rag and quietly prodded the other officer, "The dog?"

"We'll have to take the dog, Lady, to process it for evidence." His phone rang. He pulled it out of his pocket and grunted a greeting. He listened to Aunt Patty's objections and the phone while chatter spewed from both officers' radios.

"Any evidence you might have found is on that rag which I used to dry the dog before letting him in. I used a different rag for my dog. Sorry, the dog stays."

The two officers looked at each other. Officer Lewis reached for the door knob, slowing down when Mom insisted, "Don't you need a search warrant to enter our house?"

"Yes, but I can take you in for impeding an investigation."

Reluctantly she sighed, "I'll get the dog. Please stand back." With a heavy heart Mom opened the kitchen door releasing the barking dogs to the mud room. Taking Max by the collar, looking him in the eyes she ordered, "Come." Then looking at Mitzy she signaled her to stay.

Max lunged out the door jerking her behind. The officers stepped back. The rain became a downpour. Mom inquired, "Well, who's going to take him?

Looking at each other, the rag and the rain, they admitted defeat. "Oh, keep him here." Officer Minks added, "We may be back to charge you with destroying evidence," as she ran to her squad car.

She opened her window as she rode by, but Mom beat her to the punch line. "If you're charging anyone with the destruction it should be the rain." The window shot up as Mom waved goodbye and wished her a good day.

Chapter Sixteen

With a sense of satisfaction Mom came inside. I was sitting on the floor hugging the two dogs. For some reason, I had been affected by seeing the injured man. Mom's phone singing her husband's ringtone led her to her office.

"Hi, Honey."

I listened to the one sided conversation.

"Nothing. Well, no. When we went out this morning there was a body on the... I mean a person, ...a bloody person in our woods on the ground."

"No, you don't have to come home. I suppose Mrs. Jurek called to tell you the police and an ambulance were in our drive."

"Because I didn't have time. We're safe. The police were here and a detective is expected here shortly."

"And just what do you expect to do here that you can't do three hours later? Besides how often do you hold down the fort on a Saturday? They're counting on you."

I laughed to myself. I knew Mom was talking to her overprotective husband and hoped that they wouldn't start talking about me.

"Yes, and I'm not sure what to do about it."

I winced.

"No, I'll deal with it until you get home. Could you pick up some Chinese on the way home?"

"Oh, Mitzy picked up a stray who looks a lot like her."

"Does that silence mean you'll be home forthwith or at the regular time? Art, please stay at work. In a couple of hours we'll appreciate your fresh insights as well as the Chinese you'll be bringing home?"

"Thanks. Love you. See you around six."

"Right, six thirty. Thanks for picking up dinner. Love you."

As Mom hung up, I rushed by drying my eyes on my sleeve. Mom quashed her instinct to follow me. She had told Dr.Phil she felt negligent giving me the room the counselor had advised. I returned and noticed the two dogs dividing their attention between me and the back door. They wanted out. The rain had stopped. No doubt if I opened the door they would immediately zip to the crime scene. That thought escorted me to a dining room chair. Crime scene. My adrenaline level dropped and the severity of the situation surfaced. A crime had occurred on our property. Whoever did it might still be out there. Why didn't an officer stay until the detective arrived like they did on TV? Could the announcement on their radios be that urgent that both had to go?

I calmly asked, "Can we take the dogs for a walk?"

Mom worried, "Are you okay, Sara?"

"I'm angry and I don't know why?"

"Want to talk about it?"

"No," I shot back surprising myself with my intensity. "Sorry, not now."

"I'm here when you're ready if you can't find someone else to talk things through."

"I know. Thanks, Mom. Right now I just want to walk. Can I take Max?" I pleaded as I got two leashes.

"Think you can handle him?"

Max as if responding, sat at my feet, wagging his tail as I leashed him.

"What a difference since the last time. Let's go out the side door, so we're not distracted..."

"By the crime scene," I finished.

Our foursome cut through the field and almost made it to the road when my friend, Kim, came running up. "I just got home from my gram's and heard that there had been an ambulance and police at your place." Looking at me she continued, "And you were worried about today being a boring day."

An approaching red Honda civic slowed down. The driver rolled down his window inquiring, "Are you...? Oh, you're Jerry's mom."

"Right and you're Cory Watkins, no doubt looking for Patty Cowley."

"Yes, Mrs. Cowley."

"Detective Watkins, why don't you drive up to the house? I'll meet you there shortly."

He turned into the driveway.

Kim held out her hand for the dog's leash, "Mrs. C. I'll take your place walking the dog."

"Thanks, Kim. Sara, are you okay continuing the walk?"

Totally misinterpreting the question, I replied, "Of course. See Max isn't giving me any problems. He's better at heeling than Mitzy. I have my phone and will call you if we need a rescue."

"Please do, but I'm sure you girls will be fine," Mom confidently agreed as she returned home.

I felt relieved as we walked. I didn't feel like talking out my mixed emotions with my aunt even if she was my mom.

Chapter Seventeen

After walking a block in silence, Kim entreated, "Are you okay?"

I glared at Kim. Didn't she know how much I hated that question? I kicked a rock from the road into the tall grass. I fumed and didn't know why. Kim walked toward a pile of rocks by the drainage ditch and handed me one. I threw it as far as I could into a small pond. Both Max and Mitzy tried to run after it, pulling us down on top of each other, tangling us in their leashes. We started to laugh.

"Why don't I take both dogs?" Kim offered.

I handed her Max's leash and she moved to a wooded area about twenty feet away. She distracted the dogs while I threw rock after rock wishing I knew why I was so mad. Gradually, I lost the energy for throwing rocks. My anger had lessened. I joined Kim.

"Are you going to call Dr. Phil?"

I shrugged and took Max's leash. "Let's head home."

"Sara, what would Dr. Phil ask you, if she were here?"

"Something I wouldn't expect." As we continued home I realized and muttered, "Red."

"Red?" Kim wondered.

I tried explaining. "I don't like red." Hearing myself say it made me realize, "No, that's not really it." We walked a little further. "It's the blood. I didn't want to see blood here. I was mad that the blood had found me."

"The blood from the accident?"

"Yes, but that's ridiculous."

"I don't think so," Kim assured me as we approached the house and a woman standing outside.

The woman used to be my aunt but today calling her mom seemed right. She guessed, "You didn't have any problems with the dogs."

"Right, Mrs. C. and I think Sara figured out why she got so angry today."

I poked her hoping she'd regret her words.

Before I could find words to apologize, I began speaking, "I got mad when I saw the blood because it reminded me of the car accident and seeing all that blood on my brother. I am so angry at the girl who had been texting and lost control of her car. Then I got angry at myself because she lost her life too."

Kim observed, "Your flashbacks are like those my uncle has from Vietnam and my brother, Brian, has from Iraq."

"Kim, your uncle still has flashbacks?" Mom echoed.

"Yeah, Mrs. C. but he says they are getting less frequent."

"Sara, are you still angry?" Mom prompted.

"I'm still mad at the girl. But we worked through some of my anger."

"Oh?"

"Mrs. C, you know that drainage ditch down the road, the one with the pond off to the side?"

"The one by the rock pile?"

"That's the place," I confirmed. "Though we did some rearranging. After throwing those rocks with all the anger I felt, there isn't much of a pond left."

"Or rock pile," Kim added.

"Max thought he should fetch the rocks and went running after the first one dragging me behind," I admitted while brushing dirt from my jeans. "I think I'll have some bruises tomorrow. But it was worth it to get rid of that anger."

I smiled as I scrunched down embracing Max while removing his leash. My face felt relaxed. I had thrown away the tensions of the morning.

"Mom, can Kim stay for dinner?"

Mom hesitated.

"What happened to the crime tape?" I asked seeing it balled up in her hand.

"The detective took it down. The hunter fell on some kind of trap ..."

Before she could finish the dogs barked as my new brother drove up in his ancient burgundy Cavalier. They danced around him as he got out holding a brown bag. He greeted everyone and explained, "I figured with all that happened it would be a night for Chinese. I tried calling Pops but he had left the office and wasn't answering his cell phone."

"Jerry, you know your father never does when he's driving."

"Right. So I decided to pick up Chinese because I knew Pops wouldn't have gotten enough to include me. So I got enough for the whole family in case he didn't pick any up."

We headed for the house when the dogs again barked welcome, this time to Uncle Art. He parked, and then joined us. The dogs circled him sniffing the smaller brown bag he held.

Kim separated from the group, groaning, "Guess, I should be heading home for dinner."

"Please stay if it's okay with your mom," I begged.

"Thanks. Mrs. C. may I call her from your phone?"

"Here use mine," I offered while taking it from my jean pocket. "We're having Chinese so you'll get to try real Chinese, not just cafeteria chop suey."

Kim remained outside talking to her mom. She bounded in with, "Mom said I could stay."

"Great," we chorused. I handed her some silverware and the two of us finished setting the table while Jerry poured the drinks.

Chapter Eighteen

After everyone had settled down, Uncle Art offered grace. Mom added thanksgiving that our hunter, now known as Riam, was expected to recover. I explained each item to Kim and encouraged her to try a little of each.

Then Jerry interrupted, "Before we hear the story of what happened from the beginning, why are two dogs here? Sara, have you been doing cloning in sixth grade science?"

"You know, Jerry, that's not allowed until high school," I teased. "You'll find out. It's part of the story so Mom will be including it."

"I will," Mom acknowledged then continued to relate all that had happened that morning with very few interruptions from the others.

She had gotten to the arrival of the detective when Uncle Art suggested, "Patty, why don't you eat before it gets cold? Jerry, I'm sure you're here because someone called you. What did you hear?"

"I got a tweet from Wanda who probably got a call from Mrs. J. It reported, 'Cops and ambulance at your place. Jerry, hope everything's okay.' I got a couple of other text messages and decided rather than calling I would come home and check it out for myself."

Kim and I discussed which of the Chinese entrees we preferred. Mom started packing up the leftovers for

Jerry to take while Uncle Art quizzed Jerry on how his car was running.

"Girls, let the dogs out but, please, keep an eye on them," Mom requested

"Should we put them on leashes?" I inquired.

"I don't think so. Jerry, why don't you go with in case I'm wrong."

We argued that we could handle the dogs without Jerry. When we got outside Jerry explained, "Mom didn't send me out because you needed help. She and Dad need to talk about something alone. So you let the dogs run. I need to see Mr. Major across the street."

As we threw sticks for the dogs to catch, we tried guessing what they needed to talk about without us. When Jerry returned, he looked at me as if he was disappointed. He cautioned, "Sara, you shouldn't get too attached to Max. He's not ours."

I brushed him off with, "I know, I know." I turned away so my face wouldn't betray the truth. I didn't believe him. Max was mine. How could I think of giving him up no matter what proof someone had that he once belonged to them? Max returned with the stick I had thrown as the door opened.

"Dessert's ready," Mom announced.

The two dogs bounded into the house ahead of us. As we all sat at the table, Uncle Art reminded us, "We need to finish hearing about today's events." He motioned to Mom to continue.

"When the detective came I went with him to check out things. There were prints in the compost pile, the chicken coop and where the hunter had fallen."

Kim and I looked at each other, while Jerry questioned, "Prints? What kind of prints?"

Mom warned, "There may be a bear in our woods."

"Oh, there is a bear, Mr. C., Sara's bear," Kim brightly admitted.

Stunned silence. Everyone looked at me. I didn't want to say anything, but finally quietly admitted, "Yes, Dad. My bear, Bury, lives in our woods."

"We're talking about a real, wild animal, Sara," Mom stated in disbelief.

"So, Sis, you have a pet bear named Barry hanging out in the woods," Jerry chided.

In defense, Kim offered, "Berry bear is gentle and ..."

"You've seen the bear?" erupted from several directions.

"From my window at home I can see your woods. One day I saw Sarah sitting on one of the stumps in the woods with a bear next to her. That was before we met, before our camping trip. Sara told me about him on the trip after we figured out we were neighbors."

I felt trapped. I had hoped to keep Bury Bear to myself. He's like the spirit of my dead parents, not a wild animal. I added, "I didn't believe he was real until Kim told me she saw him."

"Sara, why didn't you tell anyone about the bear?" Mom scolded.

"Because he's mine," I quietly mumbled picking at the brownie in front of me. No one seemed to be eating.

Chapter Nineteen

"Mom, what does the bear have to do with what happened today?" wondered Jerry.

Mom explained, then asked, "Have any of you seen an animal trap in the woods?"

"What does it look like?" Jerry inquired.

"The detective thought it was a claw trap. Have any of you seen any trap? Better yet, Jerry were you aware of a bear in our woods? I just found out your father had suspicions and the girls have seen him."

"No knowledge of the bear," confessed Jerry as he searched the internet on his phone. "Here's a picture of a claw trap," he announced as he passed it around.

When I saw it I admitted, "We have something like that in the woods."

"Where?" urged Uncle Art as everyone got up ready to explore.

"I'll show you," I offered, relieved at the change in focus.

I took them to the edge of our property to a fallen birch tree. "There was one by this trunk but I don't see it now." I pointed to the exact spot where I had seen it. "I didn't know what it was. I thought it was just a piece of scrap metal. You could only see part of it."

After examining the area Jerry speculated, "It looks like the guy..."

"Riam, his name is Riam Vang," clarified our mom.

"Okay, Mr. Riam Vang stumbled here. See the boot tracks. He must have tripped over the log and fallen into the claw trap. That dark stuff might be his blood," suggested Jerry.

Uncle Art added, "These might be his drag marks as he walked away. Where was he found?"

"Over here," I pointed. I had moved to the place refusing to look down at the bloody leaves at my feet. I looked beyond noting that a man walking through could have caused the disturbance in the foliage.

"Here's a bear track," announced Kim two yards from me. "I'll bet Berry Bear was here. Mr. Vang saw him and fainted."

"We make a great detective team. We've got it all put together except what happened to the trap?" noted Jerry.

"Bury, probably took it off him after he fainted," I declared with confidence.

"Then what did he do with the trap?" muttered Uncle Art. I didn't think he expected an answer.

"Tossed it, would be my guess," offered Jerry. Everyone looked around.

"What's that in the tree over there?" I pointed to a shiny piece of metal about twelve feet off the ground.

Jerry reached the tree first, claiming it could be the trap. He found a sturdy branch. After cautioning everyone to move back, he pried the metal from the tree. It flipped in the air landing at Uncle Art's feet as he jumped back.

I filmed the retrieval on my phone.

"That needs to go to the detective. Wait, maybe we should have left it and had the police retrieve it," insisted Mom.

"I'm not climbing that tree to put it back," huffed Jerry. "I can drop it off at Cory's on my way home tonight. Sara, did you catch the retrieval on your phone?"

"I think I got it." Everyone gathered around me to watch the replay as I sent it to Jerry's phone.

"How about finishing dessert?" Mom suggested as we headed to the house to end a very eventful day.

My new parents couldn't agree on any action regarding the bear so did nothing. Kim and I were too busy in the gardens to bother with the woods for most of the summer. I looked forward to starting school and connecting with friends from camp. The first day of school most of the class, including Kim and me wore our tie dyed shirts from camp. I felt like I fit in more than I ever had at my old school.

Chapter Twenty

On Saturday Mom was busy preparing to go to the Twin Cities. I overheard her saying she was glad she signed up for today's Writers Workshop before we got Gina's baby shower invitation. I walked into the kitchen as Uncle Art admonished, "Patty, you were a bit harsh telling Sara she couldn't go to the baby shower before you even asked if she wanted to."

Her back was to me so she didn't notice me.

"Trust me, Art, she's not ready to go back to her old house. She hasn't been there since the accident or since Vince and Gina moved in. The baby shower would not be the best time for her first visit back."

"I still think you're wrong," Art declared while winking at me as I quietly moved closer.

Mom jumped as I greeted, "Morning, off to your writers' thing?"

"Oh, look at the time. I've got to run."

Uncle Art walked her to the door saying, "Good bye. I love you."

I waved good-bye as I poked through the fridge.

"Art, are you trying to get rid of me?" Mom questioned. He just shrugged and shook his head. She continued, "Right, you know how lost I can get. I need to start early to get lost and found and then be on time." Her voice trailed off as she got in the car.

When she drove beyond the driveway Uncle Art checked, "Okay, Sara, are you sure you want to go to Gina's baby shower?"

"Definitely. Though I do have some butterflies in my stomach about going back home."

"Okay, Sweetheart, you'll have a mix of emotions going into the house. Remember our agreement, right?"

"Yes, I will be honest with you about how I feel. If my feelings are mixed up I'll talk them through with you if you haven't gone already, or with Aunt Stella or Aunt Linda. I will," I promised. "I am excited to finally go back home. I know Gina and Vince have probably made some changes. So it won't be exactly how I remember it. That's okay. It's not my home anymore."

"Maybe going back for the first time shouldn't be on the day of the baby shower."

I glared at him in disbelief. I was more excited about going to the shower than about seeing the house that was fading from my memory. For the past eight months I had wanted to see my house again. Three previous attempts to go home were thwarted. Not this time. I felt like screaming, crying, running out the door when a paw brushed my knee. Max looked up at me, concern in his eyes, chew toy in his mouth.

I smiled took a deep breath and with a quiver in my voice declared, "Dad, I'm going to the baby shower."

"Yes, you are and you'll have fun at the shower."

Trying to swallow my deep feelings I hugged him and he reminded me, "Crying is perfectly okay. You don't have to know why you're crying. Just let yourself cry."

"Thanks," I mumbled no longer feeling like crying. Then I begged, "Can Max go with us?"

"You mean Mitzy?"

"No, Max," adding a pleading, "please."

"Well, okay. Put Mitzy on the chain by the dog house and find a leash for Max." He left out the usual warning that Max was a temporary addition until we could find his owner. I definitely had bonded to Max. He knew Max slept in bed with me from his first night.

Finishing the tasks I reported, "Mitzy's chained. She has fresh water."

50

I picked up my shower gift. Before leaving I told Dad, "Going to the shower is a little more exciting since Mom was so convinced I shouldn't."

"From time immemorial kids have played one parent against the other. You have been straining to be so good since you moved in. It's about time you got into some safe mischief."

I blushed.

"As you get more comfortable I am sure you'll find scrapes to get into. Now remember you don't have to dig out of problems alone. You have two parents who love you no matter what. If you don't think either one of us will understand, talk to your brother, or one of your cousins or teachers."

"Are you saying, Uncle Art, you want me to get into trouble?"

"No, I'm saying I want you to relax and be yourself."

"Thanks, Dad." I gave him a hug. "Everything but Max is in the car."

"Then get him loaded and we'll go."

Max hopped in.

Chapter Twenty-One

After moving to Whistlestop I went back to Elk River every day for school. No matter who drove, they refused my request to go past my old home. So finally seeing home was unreal. We pulled in the drive already filled with cars.

"You okay, Sara?" Uncle Art, no, Dad, asked.

"Not sure. For some reason I feel excited doing something Mom said I shouldn't do. Am I bad or what?"

"You're thirteen and acting like it. Vince and I are running some errands in St. Cloud. If you need me, call."

"Or, I'll talk it out with Cousin Stella."

"Good."

I clipped the leash to Max just before he jumped from the car.

Cousin Vince came out to greet us. He usually had a smart aleck greeting for me. Today words failed him. He just greeted me.

As the dog beside me growled at him, he chided, "Why is Jerry's dog, Mitzy, growling at me? Sara, have you turned her against me?" he teased. He tried taking Max's leash. The growling increased.

"Cuz, I left Mitzy at home. This is our other dog, Max. Guess he thinks I need protection from you."

"Smart dog," teased Dad.

I took the chain for the yard's dog run from my cousin and attached Max assuring him everything was okay. I pointed out the water bucket, gave him a rawhide chew and a hug. I hugged my dad and high fived my cousin in farewell.

Approaching the door of my childhood home, I reverted to my pre-accident self. As I walked in I felt at home greeting my female relatives and our friends.

When my grandmother had sold the family farm my dad had agreed to add a large room to our house for family get togethers. Many cousins, aunts and uncles helped. I installed much of the insulation and became the number one gofer on the project. While the extended family had gathered here for all major holidays, I always thought baby showers were special.

After greeting everyone, I sat down and the baby was passed to me. When the baby in my lap began to fuss, I settled him on my shoulder. He approved. I wrongly felt the whole room was focussing on the baby. Later I was told I had been the focus of everyone's concern. That's why Gina had insisted I come to the party. Twenty women and a baby serving as a distraction cushioned my return home.

"Sara, you're a natural," neighbor Lily noticed while snapping a picture with her phone. "I've got to send this to Patty."

The room erupted in, "No," with a back chorus of, "not now. Turn off that phone."

"Mrs. Backus, please don't do that," I pleaded as she pocketed her phone looking stunned. "Mom doesn't know I'm here. She didn't want me to come. You can send the photo tonight after I explain what we did. As Dad put it," lowering my voice I mimicked, 'We are a democratic household. So two votes yes overruled her no vote.'"

"Why didn't you tell her then? It's such a logical explanation?" reflected Cousin Stella.

"Because then she would spend the day worrying. She pays a lot for those Loft classes. It would be a waste for her to worry through it."

"Very thoughtful, Sara," applauded Gina.

"I'd like to see my sister's face when you dethrone her," smirked Aunt Patty's, rather my mom's sister, Aunt Diane.

53

Chapter Twenty-Two

I surrendered the sleeping Jordan to Gina to be tucked in the corner bassinet.

Aunt Pearl, the family's designated party planner, took over the shower games and opening of the baby gifts. Prizes were numbered plastic discs: the tops of peanut butter, frosting and other recycled not discarded containers. For an hour the laughter grew, while Baby Jordan slept.

When the group moved to the table for refreshments, the quieter chatter woke up the baby.

Gina retrieved him and rejoined the group. I could hear her from the kitchen wondering, "Where's Sara? Is she still in the kitchen?"

I popped my head out looking full of mischief. "I'm here. I'll be there in a minute."

I hummed as I quickly filled my plate and returned to the group.

Jovial conversation continued as plates emptied and Jordan burped. Gina and I shared conspiratorial glances. I answered Gina's raised eyebrows with a wink and a bobbing head.

"Pearl, what are we supposed to do with these?" Cousin Stella inquired holding up disc #4.

"Ask, Gina. She's in charge of prizes."

Before Gina could answer, I stood up. Gina focused her phone on me as I announced with a slight tremble in my voice, "Your prize is in the kitchen with a pink label on it." My voice strengthened as I added, "It's all junk. Well, not really." With a smile I finished, "It's extra stuff that neither Gina or I want. If you can't find something you want, after everyone has their pick, I'll pick a prize for you. So number one and two can go to the kitchen and pick."

When I saw Aunt Diane and Aunt Linda returning excited about their treasures I proclaimed, "Thanks, those were two items Mom kept putting out for garage sales and no one ever bought."

"Three and four," Gina called out.

"Five," I called out a little later. Realizing it was my number I added, "Scratch that ..."

Aunt Pearl's, "No," cut me short. Taking a package from the chair beside her she identified, "Prize number five," while handing it to me.

I ripped into the paper to a chorus of, "Open it." Time stood still has I went back to my tenth birthday and the same chorus preceded the same gift.

"A diary," my ten-year-old self declared trying to put appreciation into my disappointment at the ugly green thing with a weed and bugs on it sitting in my lap unopened.

My mother, misreading me as usual beamed, "I'm glad you like it, Butterfly." My mood had softened as I examined the Monarch and dragonflies on the cover. Opening the pages, I saw butterflies, lady bugs, a frog and other snippets of nature faintly gracing the soft green pages. I snapped the book shut when my mom mentioned, "It will be a treasure you will appreciate later in life if you write in it everyday."

"Everyday?" I moaned as if questioning a death sentence.

"Most days," my Dad advised. I thought Dad understood which CD I wanted.

This diary was different. It had a soft padded cover with a wonderful purple design. This time the gift was okay, more than okay. "Thanks. I don't have much space in my old diary."

The rest of the prizes were selected and admired. A little later I helped people get their coats and saw them off, grateful to have some time alone with Gina.

Chapter Twenty-Three

"Great party, Gina. Thanks for insisting my dad let me come."

"Thanks for your help." She was rocking the smothering farewells out of Jordan.

"I'll get the dishes," I offered not realizing that Aunt Pearl and Aunt Linda had not left.

Aunt Linda called out, "We've got it covered."

Following Gina's signal, I sat down on the couch closest to the rocking chair. I got the expected question, "How are you doing?"

With some irritation I complained, "Why does everyone ask that?"

"Because we love you and care about you. This has been a traumatic year for you. We're afraid you are overwhelmed, numbed by your parents' death," Aunt Pearl explained as she entered.

Aunt Linda added, "We're afraid that the enormity of the tragedy will hit you and we want to be there to support you through it."

I looked at the women who really loved me while debating what to say. I tried, "Okay, I haven't told anyone this, except my friend, Kim. Please don't think I'm crazy."

"Crazy is normal in the family," Aunt Pearl quipped.

I froze. Clinging to an inspired distraction I looked at Aunt Pearl and Aunt Linda and questioned what I knew I shouldn't. "Are you to going to get married now that you can?" Seeing the surprise on their faces I quickly added, "Sorry, I shouldn't have..."

"Why not?" Aunt Pearl interrupted. "We stayed behind so we could invite you to be our bridesmaid. We didn't think you knew we were a couple. You never treated us any different from the rest of the family."

"Why should I treat you differently?" I pondered, bewildered. "Yes, I will. I've always wanted to be in a wedding."

Gina noted, "Now that's taken care of, you can go back to what you were about to say?"

"I don't know where to start," I confessed.

"Do you remember the accident?" Aunt Linda prompted.

"Yes, I remember we were driving to the airport and all of a sudden a car drove into our car and crushed Mom and Dad. I yelled. Everything went black then bright white. Mother and Dad were there. I could hear them more than see them. They told me they were dead, that they loved me and I would be okay.

"Like a movie it kept on repeating over and over.

"I heard voices. I think they were the nurses or doctors. They talked around me and seemed worried. The voices kept on saying, 'wake up.' Only one person didn't tell me to do that, at least not at first. She introduced herself as the chaplain. She explained I was in a coma so my body could heal. She prayed prayers I knew.

"One day she talked about the accident. She told me that the doctors thought I was reliving it because every once and a while I would yell. My yelling was becoming less frequent and quieter. She wanted to know if I was ready to wake up.

"Someone came in the room. She introduced herself to them questioning how they were related to me. They explained I would be living with them. She asked if they had told me. They questioned her. How could they since I was in a coma?

"The chaplain told them I could still hear. Then she addressed me, 'Sara, your Uncle Art and Aunt Patty are here. When you get better you will be going home with them.'

57

"Then she suggested, 'Explain to Sara how that will happen, what living with you will be like.' They must have made a face because she added, 'No one will think your crazy. Sara needs to know what life will be like after the crash.'

"So they started to talk to me about my brother and their dog, Mitzy. That explained why Jerry and his girlfriend had been coming to see me every night. They talked and read to me. Sometimes when they did I could see my brother, Justin hanging around. Usually I saw him off playing with other kids. He seemed happy.

"Mother and Dad were with me when Aunt Patty and Uncle Art started to talk to me. Then they like faded into Uncle Art and Aunt Patty. I didn't like that because I didn't want to lose them. They explained their bodies were broken but they would always be with me in spirit.

"I started to get tired of sleeping. Once when Aunt Patty kissed me before leaving I opened my eyes. All of a sudden everything in the room started to move. People were poking me, looking in my eyes, talking about me. I went back to sleep. It wasn't the after crash sleep, rather regular sleep."

Chapter Twenty-Four

After telling them more than I had ever told anyone else, I went silent. The others relaxed into the silence. I wondered if my parents were really there when I was in the coma. They acted so much nicer than when they were alive. Aunt Pearl pulled me from my silence. "Do you still have nightmares about the crash?"

"No, if I do, I don't remember them."

"Pray tell what do you dream about?" Aunt Linda inquired.

"Bears, lots of bears, but especially Bury Bear." I tasted those words like smooth caramel.

"Whose Barry Bear?"

"Now you're really going to think I'm crazy. I think it was just before the Fourth of July when everyone agreed we would be celebrating in a park instead of back home. I got real sad. I went into the woods with Mitzy and sat on a stump. Mitzy walked off toward the well. She went up to what looked like a bear and sniffed around it. She walked back to me with the bear following."

"Were you scared?"

"No, I was too sad to be scared. Maybe it was because Mitzy wasn't scared.

Just then Max began barking. Aunt Linda offered, "Should I bring the dog in the house?"

Gina suggested, "Unleash him and let him run around and do his business before he comes in."

Aunt Linda left and I continued, "The bear had my mom's eyes. It followed Mitzy. When she sat at my feet it did too. I slid down on the ground between them. My sadness lessened as I petted the bear."

"Was this only once?"

"No, Gina, I've seen the bear five or six times. I know its real because our neighbor, Kim, has seen me with the bear."

"What did she say about it?" asked Aunt Pearl.

"Nothing. She had a hard time believing what she saw. She didn't know me. We met on a camping trip later. She told me then."

Max bounded in and up on the couch putting his head in my lap. I scolded, "Not on furniture, Max. You know better."

Gina appealed, "Oh leave him, Sara. That's one piece of furniture he can use."

"Hear that, Max. You're welcome on this couch only. No other furniture."

Max looked at me with laughing eyes. Mentally I added, "And my bed."

Chapter Twenty-Five

Uncle Art arrived as the day faded. He found me asleep on the couch using Max as a pillow. Gina and the baby were dozing in the recliner. He shook me, whispering, "Ready to head home and face the music?"

Vince entered booming, "Party over?" fully waking everyone. The baby cried. Gina glared. Vince apologized, picked up the baby and headed to check his diaper.

"Can you stay for dinner?" Gina pleaded. "We have plenty of leftovers."

"Can we, Dad?"

"Sure, your mother was going to dinner with friends after my workshop. So why not."

I went into the kitchen and helped Gina put dinner together. Vince appeared with a freshly diapered baby. We were in the middle of eating when I got a phone call. I took out my phone and noticed, "It's Mom."

"Hi, Mom. Where are you?"

"No, we're eating dinner now. Why don't you join us?"

"At Vince and..." Gina took the phone from me and walked out of the room.

I explained, "The person Mom planned on going out to eat with canceled. She thought of bringing dinner home but decided to call first. She had planned to swing by and drop off her shower gift for the baby on her way home."

Gina returned with my phone. "Your Mom should be here in fifteen minutes. She already knew you were at the shower. Pearl called her and sent her some pictures."

"Was she mad?" I winced.

"I don't know. I pretty much did all the talking and then asked if she was driving. She was so I quickly ended the call."

I took a hoagie bun and piled on leftover cold cuts and greens. "For Mom, when she gets here," I explained.

"Great idea." My dad predicted, "Knowing Patty, since we're finished eating she won't want to eat. She'll probably say she's not hungry."

Gina wrapped the sandwich just as Mom rang the doorbell and entered. "Sorry, I hope I didn't wake the baby."

"No, we told Jordan he couldn't go to sleep until he saw his Aunt Patty," Vince joked.

"Hi, Mom," I greeted while hugging her. Uncle Art kissed her. He took the gift from her hand and presented it to Gina who immediately opened it.

"Gina, I know they're size two but I figure he'll grow into them," Mom acknowledged while Gina held up bib overalls twice as long as Jordan.

"Aunt Patty, that's great. He has plenty of clothes for now. Would you like something to eat?"

"I'm not really hungry," she replied.

Uncle Art, standing behind his wife, raised his hands in an "I told you so" pose.

As we prepared to leave, Vince said, "Art, it's too dark for me to check your mystery noise tonight. If you leave your car here I could check it tomorrow and drop it by in the early afternoon. A buddy and I were planning on being in your neighbor then."

"You don't mind?"

"No problem. This way you can drive your wife's car while she eats the dinner Sara prepared."

That's exactly what we did. I was mystified as Mom and Dad discussed the day without any accusations. Mom acknowledged she was glad I had gone and apologized for trying to stop me. She also admitted being hungry and grateful for the sandwich.

62

Chapter Twenty-Six

On Monday I sprang out of the house tossing my honey hair free of its ponytail. As I closed the door behind me, I yelled at the top of my lungs, "The year of the zombie is over." I felt alive in my birthmother's blouse with its oversized monarchs. I was admiring how my orange leggings matched the butterflies when I noticed Kim, waving at me from across the street.

Kim called, "We're early enough to get the bus from here."

I joined her.

"Sara, did I hear you yelling about zombies? You look great, by the way. I take it the baby shower went well. Now, zombies, what's that about?"

"You know our Language Arts project?"

"Writing about one year in our life, that one?"

"Right. I just figured out my title - *The Year of the Zombie*."

"Last year?" Kim guessed.

I shook my head and felt a little sadness creep in but chose to ignore it. I stared at the butterflies on my blouse absorbing their joy.

"That top looks great on you. Is it new?"

"For me, yes." I wasn't sure my bubble of joy would burst by explaining it was my mother's, mother number one, that is. So I didn't. Instead I observed, "Here comes the bus."

I followed Kim who gloried in having so many seats to choose from. I was busy feeling a freeing joy that I couldn't explain but didn't want to lose.

Plopping in a choice seat, Kim exclaimed, "Sara, your weekend must have been fantastic. You glow. What happened?"

"Kim, it's like a shell broke open and I'm feeling like I used to feel before the accident."

"The one that killed your mom, dad and brother?" Kim looked at me apologetically as if regretting her words. However, unlike previous mentioning of that day, my mood didn't darken.

"Yes, I feel like a butterfly coming out of its cocoon."

"Chrysalis," Kim corrected.

"Whatever. Today is a new day with new adventures ready to begin." I explained that Gina had sent me home with some clothes of my mother's that she thought would fit me, clothes like the blouse I had on.

Then I noticed a boy entering the bus who looked like he had been crying. He took the seat in front of us with his brother, Rick.

"Justin, you okay?" I asked. I knew his name because he looked so much like my dead brother, also a Justin. The first time I saw him on the bus my heart skipped a beat and adopted him.

"No! Someone stole my dog," he sulked.

His brother immediately corrected him, "His dog ran away."

"No, Turbo, would not run away."

"When did this happen?" Kim inquired.

"Yesterday, Sunday. Matt's miniature cocker spaniel is missing too. He lives down the street from us."

Emma, who sat across from us added, "Our lab ran away. My dad claims it's because it's deer hunting season. Dogs chase deer and get lost. Some hunters shoot the dogs so they won't chase the deer. But I don't believe that. I'm with Justin. Someone is stealing our dogs."

"Have you seen any strange vans around your house?" Kim wondered.

Her question surprised me.

"Come to think of it," Justin remembered, "there's been a grey van parked around. We figured they were deer hunting."

Kim sorted through some pictures in her purse. She pulled one out. "Did it look like this?"

"Yeah, that looks like it. I noticed the half peeled off Obama sticker. I hadn't noticed the missing license plate," explained Justin.

"Kim, why do you have the picture?"

"It's from last year, Sara. I noticed it at the start of the bow hunting season. It looked suspicious."

"Let me see that picture," insisted Rick. "Yeah, I've seen that van around with two guys I wouldn't want to meet in a dark alley. The windows were so dark it's hard to see if anyone is inside. So maybe we have a dog stealing ring. Should we call the police?"

"Lisa Olsen did that last year," Emma sighed.

"Did the police do anything?" I asked.

"No, they apologized saying they had too many real crimes and didn't have time to look for a lost dog," Emma sadly noted.

"We do!" I declared looking into Kim's eyes for confirmation.

The air was electric with possibilities for rescuing dogs. Like spontaneous combustion, an organization was birthed with Kim announcing, "The Kimsara Detective Agency will get to the bottom of this."

Chapter Twenty-Seven

Detective Agency - hadn't my dad, my first dad, told me I would be a great detective someday? I didn't remember sharing that information with Kim. A feeling that I was where I should be led me to address the kids near us, "We'll need everyone's help. Get a list of any missing dogs in your neighborhood. Talk to kids at school. See if they have seen the grey van or are missing dogs. Are you with us?"

Everyone was. The bus had reached school.

"Together we will stop the dog stealing," I promised. All agreed.

As the bus emptied, Kim and I sat transfixed wondering what we had just done. The bus driver, two seats ahead, turned back commenting, "Boy, I sure hope you get them. I think our neighbor's dog ran away. I'll get the details and give them to you. I'll also post a note on the bus driver's bulletin board. How should they contact the Sarakim agency?"

I corrected him, "That's Kimsara. Here's an email address that you can use after tomorrow morning." I handed him a post-it note with kimsara@whistlestop.net before departing the bus.

"How do you know that's available?" inquired Kim. She had read the note as it passed by her.

"My phone has internet. So I checked. I think you have to be over eighteen to set up an address. I'll see if

Uncle Art, I mean, Dad or Mom can set it up tonight," I promised while stepping off the bus. "See you later."

The school day flew by. On the way home Kim and I talked about the missing dogs with the others on the bus. Gathering facts, we failed to get off the bus the first time it passed our houses. On the second approach the driver called out, "Are you detectives going back to school with me?"

We shot off the bus and separated to our respective homes.

I knew neither parent would be home. I unchained our two dogs and let them run free while I quickly changed. I stuffed two apples in my pockets, grabbed two leashes and went outside. No dogs. My heart sank. Our dogs couldn't have been stolen. I plopped down on the steps, then smiled as the two dogs ran to me from the woods.

Had they read my mind? I definitely wanted them to run around the woods rather than take them for a walk. My heart leapt as I ran to the dark figure, my bear, who sat on a downed trunk. I looked into its maternal brown eyes and hugged it. The dogs played their tag-like game around us. I held out an apple to the bear and gushed about how great I felt. I sat on a stump I had maneuvered so we sat almost eye to eye.

As I spoke Bury Bear looked pleased and accepted the apple I offered. We ate. I offered it my apple core. I then moved next to Bury resting my head on its shoulder.

Soon Bury moved. After a quick hug I started toward the house. Canine barks announced the arrival of my mother. I joined her. As we walked into the house I explained the Kimsara Detective Agency. She agreed to set up our email account after dinner.

Chapter Twenty-Eight

The next morning I found two sets of business cards on the kitchen table, one for me and one for Kim. "Thanks, Mom," I squealed, hugging her as she entered the kitchen.

"I used my P.O. Box until you get an income and can rent your own."

"I doubt we'll get any mail."

"You never know."

I inhaled breakfast and made it to the early side of the bus route before Kim. I handed Kim her business cards when she arrived. We found a dozen ways to say we couldn't believe we were a detective agency before we reached school.

At lunch Kim and I found an empty table. A lanky boy in jeans and a button down khaki shirt approached. He began, "Is this the detective agency that's going to find out why the dogs are disappearing?"

"Yes, we are the Kimsara Detective Agency," I proclaimed with pride. "Can we help you?"

Confidently he announced, "Maybe I can help you. Is this the van you're looking for?" He handed me his cell phone.

"I think so. Do you have it from different angles?" asked Kim.

"Do I ever? I have been suspicious of this van so I have documented every time I saw it in my neighborhood. I

68

have the dates and the times. With my name, I expect to be a detective someday."

"Your name?" I inquired.

"Well, I suppose I should introduce myself. I'm RT, short for Richard or Dick Tracy. I'm in eighth grade and would love to join your agency."

"I'm Sara and this is Kim. We just made up the agency yesterday. We are determined to stop the dog stealing before ours get stolen."

"Dick Tracy, like the comic book detective?" quipped Kim.

"Right, so you see why I go by RT." He pulled out his business card from his wallet. "Text me tonight. I don't keep all my pictures on my phone. I've downloaded them to a file that I'd be happy to share. Gotta go. Nice meeting you two."

When he left we noticed that the table had filled with several from the bus. Justin handed me a torn piece of notebook paper saying, "Here's a list of dogs that have disappeared recently. No one remembered the van."

Emma pouted, "I hope you find our dogs."

"My brother told me to be realistic. Our dogs are probably sold by now," lamented Justin to bring the group back to a reality he did not want to believe.

RT returned to the table handing me another business card. "I just remembered. When we had career day, this officer came out. She does IT for the county sheriff and encouraged us to contact her if we have any questions about getting into law enforcement. Thought your agency might want a cop contact."

"Thanks, RT. It might be helpful," I admitted. I took a picture of the card and handed it back as the ringing bell ended lunch.

On the bus ride home, Kim apologized, "I hope you don't mind my name being first."

"No, Kimsara sounds a lot better than Sarakim. Can you believe what we have done?   Doesn't it sound exciting?" I exclaimed while texting my email address to RT.

Chapter Twenty-Nine

As we approached home, Kim gasped, "The van, the grey van," while pointing out the window.

Once off the bus, we ran to my house. Rushing in breathlessly I pleaded, "Mom, can we take the dogs for a walk?"

"Now?" she questioned.

"Yes, Mrs. C.. When we get back we'll explain everything."

"Okay, get home before dinner."

"We will." The dogs, seeing their leashes out, leapt with joy.

"Okay," I cautioned, "we've got to act natural. I don't think we'll want to get too close to it."

As we passed the dark windowed van on the other side of the street, Max growled. "That's the first time I've heard him growl since that day we found him."

About fifteen feet past the apparently empty van I said, "Here take Max's leash. I want to get a picture of the two dogs."

Kim knowing what I wanted, poised the dogs with their backs to the van. I took a couple of pictures including one of the front license plate.

Looking at her watch Kim announced, "It's almost dinner time."

We hurried past the van and back into the house. We explained everything. Mom cautioned us not to approach the van again.

I changed the subject saying our email address was working and she suggested we put together a website under our company name which she had obtained for us.

"Kim, won't your mother be looking for you by now?" Mom cautioned.

"Oh, right, Mrs. C.. I'm so excited."

"Both of you better calm down and get your homework done."

"Bye, see you tomorrow, Sara."

"Yes, at the Kimsara office," I replied.

After dinner, I flew through my homework. Then I followed RT's lead using the email address from the card he gave me.

Dear Officer Lee Petersen, IT Specialist:

Eighth grader, RT, gave me your information because he thought you could help us. We believe someone is stealing the dogs in our neighborhood. It happened last year at the same time. Many parents claim the dogs are running off after the deer. But we don't believe it.

We think the people who are stealing the dogs use the van in the picture I enclosed. There is a license plate on the front but none on the back. We are gathering information on where and when the van has been seen, and which dogs disappeared that day. Last year when this happened and the police were called but they were too busy to look for lost dogs.

Can you help us? Do you want more pictures that kids took of the van or pictures of the dogs who are missing? We know that the dogs may have been sold already but we want to stop the dog thieves before more dogs are taken.

Any information or suggestions would be appreciated.

Thank you.

Sara Cowley
Kimsara Detective Agency

I forwarded copies to Kim and RT. before working on my language art project. Soon my computer announced new mail. I opened it.

Sara Cowley:

RT alerted me to a possible email from you. He noted you are seventh graders. Is that true? If so, you are very precocious to want to catch the dog thieves. That could be dangerous. Please do not approach the van. I will check our data bases on lost dogs and check out the van license.

You can send me the information you gather and I'll work with you.

I look forward to someday meeting you and learning more about the Kimsara Detective Agency.

Lee Petersen
IT Specialist.

After forwarding the letter, I texted Kim. She offered to put together our Kimsara Detective Agency Website after she got her homework finished. I went to bed excited and tired.

Chapter Thirty

I woke up thinking about the Kimsara Detective Agency. I snagged a bagel and turned on the computer surprised by the number of emails. Many kids were invested in finding the dog thieves. They had searched family pictures and emailed us several. About 25 dogs were identified as disappearing between this and last year's hunting season.

I looked up at the clock, amazed how the time had flown. I grabbed my books and dashed to the bus just as it was about to pull away. As I settled next to Kim I caught my breath.

"Wow, Sara. You cut that close."

"I know. I made the mistake of reading emails. How did so many get our email address?"

"I sent it to everyone in the school whose address I had and told them to pass it on."

"Many kids are sending us information. I forwarded it to RT to keep him in the loop. He seems interested in being part of Kimsara Detective Agency. Do you think he'll want his name added to the agency's name?"

"Let's ask him," Kim suggested as we settled into last minute review for the day's classes.

At lunch right after Kim sat down, RT joined us. He handed each of us a sheet of paper with a chart of missing dogs and van sitings.

"Very impressive," I complimented. "We're going to have to add your name to the Agency."

"Don't you dare!" RT demanded with unexpected intensity.

"Why not?" Kim wanted to know.

"Look, since I being born into the Tracy family and having a grandfather named, Richard, I got the name Richard Tracy. I never like the name Richard. So I became Dick. Now with the revival of the Dick Tracy comics my name has been my..."

"Albatross?" I offered.

"Right, my albatross. I really like working on finding who's stealing the dogs. I feel people are saying because of my name I have to become a detective. I think that's what I want to do. But I don't want my name to dictate what I do with my life."

We thought in silence until Kim prodded, "What's your middle name?"

"Cuthbert, another lame name."

Kim and I looked at each other wide-eyed at our shared insight. Kim nodded to me. I suggested, "RT, the Kimsara detective agency would like you to come aboard as our IT genius?"

Kim, reinforced it with, "RT head of IT for Kimsara. How does that sound?"

"I like it. I am so bored with school and video games, I'd love to help out."

Chapter Thirty-One

I saw classmate, Abdi, approaching and waved him to join us. "Abdi, thanks for the emails. How did you get our email address?"

"I guessed. The first three didn't go through but I lucked out on my fourth guess." Despite his dark complexion he blushed. "I am so sorry. I know you are Kim and Sara but I have a hard time remembering who's who."

"I'm Sara," I confessed.

Abdi as if creating a mental peg, echoed, "Sara, strawberry blonde."

"So, of course she's Kim. Abdi, do you know RT?" I gestured to the boy beside me.

"Should I? Is he new to the school?"

RT laughed, "No. I'm in eighth grade and usually sit on the other side of the cafeteria."

"Good to meet you, RT," Abdi said while extending his hand.

"Thanks for the emails, Abdi. Reading them almost got me late for school," I admitted.

"Sorry."

"Don't be. I'm the one who should have watched the clock. RT, I hope you didn't mind that I forwarded them to you."

"I was honored to get them. You'll notice Abdi's information is included in the graph."

I shared my graph with Abdi who entreated, "What next?"

"Good question," I answered. Silently we contemplated possibilities while eating.

Kim broke the spell with, "I think we have enough to take to the police."

"RT, you have your lap top with you. Don't you?" I stated.

"Yeah. Got some IT for me to do, Sara?"

"Yes, if you would. Could you send the collection of material to your friend at the Sherburne County Police Department? Find out what we should do next. Let her know that your data shows that most of the dogs disappeared during deer hunting seasons. So we need to act quickly."

"I have Math next. Usually when I finish my work, Mr. T lets me use my computer. WiFi reception is great in that classroom. I'll get it done. I've got to go." As he got up he winked while saying, "You can count on RT staying on top of IT."

Chapter Thirty-Two

When I got home from school my expected email from Lee Petersen had arrived telling me the van had been stolen three years ago. Then it was white. So it had been painted. She also warned the us not to approach the van again. I forwarded the email to Kim and then found my Zombie file to work on my writing assignment. So far I had written:

I didn't expect sixth grade to be my zombie year, but it was. It started normal. It was my seventh year attending Elk River Schools. My younger brother was in fourth grade. My father was a salesman who traveled a lot. My mom was an interior decorator who worked at Big Lake Lumber selling lumber and answering decorating questions.

We planned a family trip for most of January. Dad kept the destination a mystery, saying it might change because for him it would still be a business trip. My brother, Justin, and I were supposed to get our January school work done while we traveled.

When my teachers found out, most of them gave me extra work in December so I could get it done ahead of time and enjoy our traveling. I did most of my assignments before Christmas. I even worked ahead in a few of the classes.

Christmas and New Year's were exciting. Everyone came to our house for parties and tried to get my dad to tell them where we were going. He wouldn't.

We knew we were going out of the country because we all got passports. We weren't supposed to tell anyone about them.

On January 6th on the way to the airport we were in an accident.

I debated on how to describe the accident. When I heard steps in the hall I called, "Aunt Patty, I mean, Mom."

"Yes, Dear." She walked into the room and sat on the one uncluttered chair. She couldn't see the computer screen.

"I'm working on my Language Arts project."

"The Year of the Zombie?"

"Yes, that one. I'm writing about the accident. However, I don't remember much."

"If the story is from your point of view that's all you have to say."

"But, Mom, I want to know more about the accident and I can't find anything about it on the internet."

"There was very little newspaper coverage. A lot happened in the world that day."

I had a gnawing question but was afraid of the answer. I decided to risk it. "Mom, was my Dad a crook?" I stared at her with laser focus.

"Why do you say that?" she quizzed. I realized my face might register I thought he was.

"When I went back to school, kids talked. They wanted to know what my dad did for a living."

"What did you say?"

"What he told us. He was a salesman who sold widgets and wow for small companies all around the world."

"Did you believe that?"

"I wanted to but...," my voice faded. Tears welled up in my eyes.

Chapter Thirty-Three

Mom moved closer and hugged me. "Would it have been easier if he showed you the widgets he sold?"

"Yes, that's it." I pulled away and stood. "That's exactly it." I paced the room. Anger replaced my tears. I continued, "When I would ask him what specifically he sold, he would say it was proprietary information."

"Proprietary?"

"Yes, when I asked him what that meant he told me to look it up, which I did. The definition didn't help. I showed it to him and repeated my question. He explained that companies trusted him with their secrets and so he had to protect them by not talking about them."

Mom interrupted, "Your father, my brother-in-law, always had an air of mystery about him. Are you including him in your essay?"

"No, I hadn't planned on it."

"So, this is one of those writing distractions I talked about. May I suggest you open another file, your "dad" file, and put all your questions and ideas in that? You can research them another day when you're finished writing about your zombie year."

"Okay," I reluctantly sighed before I returned to the computer.

Mom stood and as she left the room offered, "I think I have the one newspaper article on the accident. I'll get it for you."

I floundered on what to write next. I recalled that when I explained my coma experience, Aunt Linda and

Aunt Pearl had acted like my story made sense. Would it make sense to my teacher and classmates? Were my parents really there when I was in the coma or were they just in my imagination?

Mom startled me. She just appeared in the doorway inquiring, "Does skipping the details of your dad help?"

"Yes, and no. He might be easier to explain than what it's like in a coma. Did you find the article?"

"It did but as you can see it has very few details and some of those are wrong." She handed me the small clipping.

I remarked, "I see what you mean. It says three died at the scene of the accident and the daughter died shortly after reaching the hospital. Didn't anyone tell the paper they were wrong?"

"Several of us did. They agreed to print a correction when space allowed. However, no one saw the correction."

"The article has Dad's name and mentions his wife, daughter and son without saying our names. Is that because we had changed our names?"

In surprise, Mom entreated, "When?"

"Just before we were going on that mystery vacation. We changed our names so everyone except Dad had Mom's maiden name."

"Did your dad say why?"

"There had been a mistake on our passports and he claimed it was easier for us to change our last names than to get new passports in time to leave. Mom argued with Dad about that."

I looked at Mom while thinking: *I didn't die. What's that about?*

Mom must have realized my mind had wandered. She tried to bring me back. "So you can't give many first hand details of the accident. Why don't you try telling how you felt after you came out of the coma and came here?" Then she looked at her watch. "It's almost dinner time. I better get cooking."

"Need some help?" I begged.

"Not as much as you need time to write. You have an hour. See what you can get done. If you want we can go over it after dinner."

Chapter Thirty-Four

Mom left before I could reply. So I returned to my writing.

I was in a coma for about a month after the accident. It was like living with curtains around me. I could hear what people were saying but I couldn't see anyone. I knew my mom, dad and brother were dead. I dreamt about them talking to me and saying goodbye. I didn't want to wake up because I knew my family was gone.

But I did wake up. Life was kind of foggy. I went to physical therapy in the hospital because some parts of my body weren't connecting with my brain. I would stumble or couldn't remember the name of some things. When I got out of the hospital I came to live with my mom's sister, Patty Cowley and her husband, Art Chaffins.

Everyday one of my new parents or my new brother would drive me to school in Elk River instead of the school in Whistlestop where we now lived. Sometimes I would go to physical therapy before or right after school. I didn't stay after school for many activities. I was too tired when the school day ended. I often slept on the way home.

Since we had been planning on a month long vacation I was ahead in my school work. That was lucky because once I got back to school it took me a while to remember stuff.

I went back to the same school building, the same homeroom, but school was different. At first my friends made a big fuss over me and helped me. Unfortunately I couldn't keep up with them. They asked so many questions. Every once and a while I would cry for no reason. At first, every time I saw one of my dead brother, Justin's, friends I would cry. Sometimes they did too. I was a mess.

Doctor Philomena Hughes helped put me together. I first met her in the hospital. She promised she would help me get out of the fog. She met with me once a week. I call her Dr. Phil like the guy on TV that my mom used to watch before she died. Dr. Phil let me talk about how I felt out of focus and weird. She suggested it might be best if I went back to my old school after the accident. After a month back at school I told her going back was a mistake. She asked me if I wanted to change schools. I did and I didn't. So I stayed there.

By the end of the school year I wasn't as clumsy. School work got easier. I had made some new friends. I wasn't going to physical therapy anymore. I had become the kid who lost her family in the car accident. I wasn't myself. I spent a lot of time alone, being sad. I was not looking forward to summer vacation. I lived in the country. I helped in the garden...

"Sara, dinner's ready."

I saved my file. I had over 700 words on the assignment requiring at least 1,000 words. I bounded down the stairs happy with what I had written. I also realized I was happy with my life.

I surprised my Uncle Art standing near the bottom of the stairs with a hug. "Hi, Dad, glad you're home." All of a sudden the ritual between me and my birthfather seemed to fit with my new dad.

Mom observing her husband's confusion and my delight suggested, "I take it your writing went well."

"Sure did. I'm almost done," I boasted while getting a pitcher of water and pouring it into glasses. We sat down to a delightful dinner.

Chapter Thirty-Five

The next Saturday I donned my monarch blouse, orange leggings and rain coat. I was meeting with Dr. Phil. Mom was uncharacteristically quiet during the wet drive. I read through the pages of information Abdi and RT had posted on the Kimsara website about dog losses in our neighborhoods.

As the car approached Dr. Phil's office, Mom finally spoke. "It's been a month since you met with Dr. Phil, hasn't it?"

"Yes, I've graduated from the weekly meetings. Today I have so much to talk about. Are you staying or running errands while we meet?"

"Staying. I brought my lap top." She parked in front of the cozy brick house and pulled out her laptop. We walked into the house, triggering the ringing of bells. Mom settled into a chair by the entranceway window.

I continued in as Dr. Phil opened her office door. She waited for me. I surprised her with a hug as I greeted her. We settled into chairs a few feet from each other.

"Sara, you look radiant."

"I feel great, like a weight has been lifted from me; like I'm back to being myself."

"When did this change begin?"

I cradled my chin in my hand and thought.

After a few moments of silence, Dr. Phil suggested, "The baby shower. Did you persuade your mother to let you go to the baby shower?"

"No."

"So you didn't go to the shower?"

"No, I went to the shower. Dad took me. Mom was afraid I wasn't ready to go back to my home. I think she felt she should go with me."

"Did you feel you were ready?" Dr. Phil prodded.

"I didn't think about going home as much as I really wanted to go to Gina's shower. Aunt Pearl let me help with the planning. Gina and I text each other at least once a day.

All of a sudden I was reliving the day of the shower, sharing details with Dr. Phil as the day played out in my mind. "Dr. Phil, when I stood in the doorway of the house where I grew up, I felt like my pre-accident self. The guy I hugged goodbye was no longer Uncle Art but my dad. My cousins, aunts and the other women at the shower treated me the same as they have done for every holiday since I was born."

"The same?" Dr. Phil noted.

"For the first time since the accident I didn't feel everyone was walking on eggshells, treating me like a bubble about to burst."

"Your father must have been quite confident you were ready to return home."

"Hardly. Cousin Vince reported Dad almost came back."

"But he didn't?"

"Right, he didn't because Cousin Vince gave him his phone which had a live feed of me at the party. I was holding the baby and laughing. So they left and ran their errands."

"This air of confidence started on that day, right. Did it last when you got home?"

"Yes, and then the next day my neighbor, Kim, and I created the Kimsara Detective Agency. Oh, yes, and I'm going to be a bridesmaid when my Aunt Linda and Aunt Pearl get married."

"Detective Agency?"

"Yes, dogs are being stolen and we're going to stop the thieves."

"You sound very confident. When you say, 'we,' who are you including?"

"Everyone. I mean we call it the Kimsara Detective Agency." I pulled out my business card and handed it to Dr. Phil. "At first it was me and my neighbor, Kim. Then about a dozen kids who lost their dogs joined us. We have an eighth grader as our IT guy. Our website has the details so people can help us. We also have a contact at the county sheriff's office."

"I look forward to hearing more about your detective work next month."

Chapter Thirty-Six

Dr. Phil noted, "You definitely have grown a lot this month. May I suggest you get back to writing in your journal?"

"I won a new journal at the baby shower. So you're not the only one thinking that. I'll bring it next month. I got my old diary from home. I was so disappointed when my parents gave that one to me."

"Did you tell your parents?" Dr. Phil inquired.

"Of course not. My mother thought I loved it. She told me if I wrote in it every day it would be a treasure later in my life. Now I wish I had."

Dr. Phil prodded, "What do you think would have happened if you were honest and told your mother you really didn't want the diary?"

"I couldn't do that. Mom and Dad fought so much that would have started a fight."

"Do your new parents fight as much?"

I thought for a while before deciding, "They don't really fight. When Mom decided I shouldn't go to the baby shower Dad disagreed. If they talked more about it, I didn't hear them."

"Sara, it's okay to disagree with your parents. It's part of growing up." She repeated herself, "You sure have grown this month."

"Wait a minute, Dr. Phil. You want me to fight with my parents?"

"No, be honest with your parents. Don't avoid honesty just because you want to avoid a fight. Does that make sense?"

"I guess," I mumbled as chimes indicated the session was over.

After setting a date for the next session, we walked out of the office together. Mom was still typing in the foyer. Rain fell heavier than before. Mom looked up, "Sara, you look like you're up to some mischief."

"Dr. Phil said mothers and daughters are supposed to fight." Noting the shocked expression on both women, I clarified, "That didn't come out right. Let me try again." Motioning towards Mom I restarted, "I should be honest with you, Mom, especially when I think you are not going to like what I have to say."

"Oh, yes," Mom exclaimed with relief. "I sometimes feel you are saying what you think I want to hear."

I blushed.

She continued, "That's so hard to deal with."

Dr. Phil continued, "Patty, what would have happened if she had told you she really wanted to go to the baby shower?"

"I probably would have let her go."

"Really, Mom?"

"Yes, your father wanted you to go. Several of the women attending the shower called me the day I told Gina you wouldn't be there. They all insisted you should be there. I even thought of not going to the workshop so I could go with you. However, you seemed content not to go."

"You never asked me if I wanted to go."

"I know. I'm sorry about that. I'm so glad Art didn't listen to me. Next time you want to do something, please speak up."

"And you'll let me do it?" I teased skeptically.

"Maybe. I'll listen to your reasons. I'll give my opinions. We'll discuss it."

Dr. Phil continued, "And who has the final decision?" Mom and I compassionately looked at each other and shrugged our shoulders.

Dr. Phil tried a different approach. "Patty, when you and your husband disagree, who has the final say?"

"I guess we make decisions by default. We each give our opinion. If we disagree we don't make a decision right away. Over the next couple of days whoever feels stronger about the issue offers more reasons and kind of wears down the other person down."

"So it's not the person who yells the loudest or cries the hardest, or ..."

I stopped Dr. Phil with, "No, they don't fight. My birthparents fought. I hated that. I have to remember that my current parents don't fight." Buoyed by a sense of security I hugged Dr. Phil and left with my mom.

Chapter Thirty-Seven

The next day, in the car on the way to Sunday services I proposed my well rehearsed question, "We're going to Vince and Gina's for Thanksgiving, aren't we?"

"Do you want to?" Dad countered.

"Of course, Gina is counting on us coming."

Mom assured me, "We've gone to the family Thanksgiving and Christmas gatherings every year so I don't see any reason for changing that. I'm surprised, Sara, you're thinking so far in advance. Do you have any plans for Halloween?"

"No, I used to take my brother, Justin, trick or treating in our neighborhood. What do you do?"

"We usually go to the adult party at the Whistlestop Tavern. The kids have parties at school and church. The only trick or treating is done as trunk or treating in the church parking lots the weekend of Halloween."

As we pulled into the church parking lot I waved, "That's Matt. He lost his miniature cocker spaniel to the thieves. The police are beginning to believe us that the dogs are being stolen. But the van seems to have disappeared."

"Maybe they got a different vehicle," offered Mom as we got out of the car.

Dad added, "Or they painted the old one."

"At least dogs aren't disappearing, which is a good thing. The thieves could have moved to some other place;

which is disappointing. We had hoped they would be caught quickly while they still had some of our dogs," I explained as I joined my parents in greeting others who were entering the church.

I was getting used to going to church every week. Previously my parents had taken me to a variety of churches a few times a year. Today I knew and liked all the songs we sang. When the service ended I gathered with some friends in the youth room until I got a text message from my dad: "ready 2 go?" I texted that I was.

When we gathered at the car, Dad checked, "Did you sign up for putting the Thanksgiving baskets together?"

"Yes, and I signed up to sing carols at the nursing home. Is that okay? I wasn't sure if I should check with you first."

Mom tried to be tactful, "If your parents were alive would you have asked them?"

After a pause, I offered, "I wouldn't have signed up for anything because I never felt part of the churches we occasionally attended. We weren't involved like you."

"How do you feel about your parents not going to church every week?" Dad prodded cautiously.

Without any hesitation I sighed, "Andy Parta said my parents are in hell because we didn't go to church every Sunday."

With a gasp, Mom queried, "Do you believe him?"

"No, of course not. I know my parents are in heaven. As my dad used to say: 'God's not a nit-picker or bean counter.'" I imitated my dad's voice until my voice cracked as the pain of missing him stung me.

"You miss them don't you?" Dad could see my emotions prevented me from verbalizing so I nodded. "You're feeling the pain of missing them right now, aren't you? It's okay to cry."

"No, you're not supposed to cry in front of people," I reasoned while gaining my composure.

Dad's comeback, "What idiot said that?" shocked me to laugh. "That's just an urban legend. Cry when you need to. Don't listen to anyone who tells you to stop. Tell them you haven't finished watering your healing."

"Very well put, Art," Mom complimented. Expanding her appreciation she added while writing in her ever present notebook, "Mind if I steal that?" We both knew Dad's response was irrelevant. He was proud when he read his words in Mom's work.

"Yeah, that was good," I paused to decide whether the next word should be "Dad," or "Art." Dodging the decision I changed the subject. "Did anyone take the dogs for a walk before church?"

"Are you offering to walk the dogs?" Mom asked.

I thought she might not want to share her morning ritual, but continued, "I'd like to walk Max. I'm not sure I could handle both?"

"Neither am I," Mom admitted as we got out of the car. "How about doing it together?"

"I'd really like that. I'll go change clothes," I agreed. Opening the door to the house released two energized streaks of fur.

"I'll make lunch," Dad volunteered. "I feel guilty that I no longer take my turn cooking during the week."

"I'm not stopping you," Mom insisted. "Though it is nice that we can eat earlier and I must say that I do enjoy cooking."

Chapter Thirty-Eight

Minutes later Mom and I each escorted a dog down the drive and on to the road. Mom asked, "What are you doing for Halloween?"

"Nothing."

"What's Kim doing?"

"She's going to the party at the Christian Center."

"You two have become inseparable since your camping trip, didn't she invite you to go with her?"

"Yes, but I don't want to go."

"Why not?"

"It doesn't sound like fun. Besides, I don't have a costume."

"That is not a problem."

We had reached an intersection. The dogs were straining to follow the well worn deer path. Mom and I examined the deer tracks, allowing the dogs a little roaming space. I tapped her shoulder then pointed to a rabbit on the other side of the intersection. We turned and urged the dogs homeward.

When we entered the house Dad announced, "Lunch is ready." The table had been set, drinks poured and a chef salad served. As lunch ended the conversation returned to Halloween. I again lamented, "I don't have a costume."

Dad responded, "Correction, you haven't picked your costume. Patty, take this young lady to the trunk."

I followed Mom upstairs to a huge cedar chest. She removed the bolts of quilting material from the top. Opening the chest and pulling out a bundle of deep red, Mom decided, "This one's out. You don't want to dress like the devil for the church party. Here, you can be a gypsy, or a pirate, or a cat." She held out a bundle for each.

"That little bundle has a whole cat outfit in it?" I questioned.

"Oh, no. You have to add a grey pullover and gray sweats." Rummaging further, Mom prompted, "You've got brown sweats and a dark green top don't you?"

"Yes," I admitted with caution not wanting to commit myself to the unknown.

Mom held up a jagged green triangle. She slipped it over my head despite my trying to wiggle away.

"Hold still," Dad commanded. "This one you have to see to believe."

I let Mom straighten the costume. She asked, "Where are the batteries?"

While Dad went to get batteries, Mom pinned some ornaments to the cloth. I didn't know whether to feel captured or loved. When Dad returned, he inserted the batteries into the costume and lights came on. I was escorted to the full length mirror and exclaimed, "A Christmas tree."

"Now this costume used to have the regular Christmas lights. So you had to stand by an outlet and plug yourself in to get the full effects. However, last year after Christmas we found these battery run lights on sale and decided they might work."

I concluded, "Mom, you were planning to wear this, right?"

"No, she wasn't. Your mother," Dad paused and watched me for some reason. I was getting more comfortable accepting them as my parents. "Your mother, is the keeper of the chest. Costume making in our Halloween group got out of hand. Each year costumes became more elaborate."

96

"Ridiculously elaborate. So I suggested we stop doing costumes. However everyone liked dressing up. So as a compromise we pooled our costumes. I volunteered to hold some of them in this cedar chest. Judith has the rest. Occasionally someone gets a novel idea or finds a new costume which we add to the collection. However most from our group will come over a few days before Halloween and create a costume from what Judith and I have. I don't pick my costume until Halloween Day using what is left over."

Dad interjected, "And yours, Dear, is always the best." He kissed his wife and went downstairs to do dishes.

Chapter Thirty-Nine

"Sara, you can be a Christmas tree, if you like. Look through the chest and see if there is something you like better. Most of the bundles are labeled. You can't say you don't have a costume. You just need to figure out if you want to go with Kim to my church's party or the one held at the school."

"Thanks, Mom," I said while exploring other parcels of material and accessories.

"You don't have to decide today. Halloween is over two weeks away. However, if you find a possible costume, put it in your room so no one else claims it. Judith has more costumes if you don't like any of these. I'm going help your father finish the dishes."

After looking through the trunk I called Kim and invited her over. When she arrived I asked her, "What are you going to be for Halloween?"

"My costumes are lame. Usually I am a bum or a zombie. Why?" Kim moaned as we headed upstairs. Her eyes widened as she saw costumes strewn around the trunk.

"When I said I wouldn't go to the party at your church because I didn't have a costume, my mom pulled out all these choices."

Kim had slipped into an azure gown and waltzed in front of the mirror as Mom approached. "Kim, you're welcome to pick a costume from the trunk if you wish."

"Mrs. C., this dress is so lovely. Thank you. With costumes like these, Sara, we should go to the party at school."

"Why not the one at the church, Kim?" Mom wanted to know.

"It's a bit boring. I go because no one cares what you wear. Most don't even bother with a costume."

"Sara, your father and I are going over to the Millers to play cards. We'll have dinner there."

"Sara can come to my house for dinner, Mrs. C.," Kim volunteered immediately regretting it. I knew her father could be hostile if his football team didn't win.

"Or, you could fix a pizza from the freezer, make sandwiches or a salad and eat here," Mom proposed.

"Don't worry, Mom. We won't starve. Have fun playing cards." I hugged my mom and returned to exploring the chest. Once it was empty we had set aside two gowns, the Christmas tree, a dog and a police costume. These we moved to my closet after repacking the rest.

After a couple of video games, hunger drove us to the kitchen. While pulling things from the refrigerator, I handed Kim my phone. "Look at the tweets from the last couple of days. Kids have seen the van and immediately reported it."

As Kim read, I commented, "But the police never get there in time. The last sighting was yesterday."

As we microwaved an assortment of leftovers, the smell of barbecue called the dogs to empty their filled dishes. Kim left as Mom and Dad returned.

Chapter Forty

The next day at lunch the Kimsara regulars gathered, lamenting how the thieves kept eluding the police. "I think they're listening in to the police calls," I conjectured.

"Lee thinks the same," RT added as he sat down.

"Should we stop calling the police, RT?" prompted Abdi.

"No, the police are going to send the information we give them to the squad car computer instead of using the radio."

"The Kimsara website has some van sitings posted for Friday but none on Saturday. I submitted one on Saturday but it's not on the website," complained Justin.

"That's because I put a filter on our site," RT admitted. "The police think the thieves have found our website. So, sorry, no one can post directly to the sight, even if you have the access codes. The postings come to me and then I post them as long as they don't alert the thieves."

Emma commented, "Is that why Kim and Sara's pictures were removed?"

Seeing our surprise, RT apologized, "Sorry, I should have told you before I removed your pictures. Officer Lee advised it in case the thieves are checking the website. Having your pictures posted could put you in danger. Once the thieves are caught, I'll put your pictures back."

"Does that mean you don't expect Kimsara to investigate anything criminal in the future?" I stated boldly trying to mask my disappointment. Without giving RT a chance to answer I continued, "We definitely should talk about it before the pictures are put back. Kimsara is more than the two of us. So we would need a group picture. Maybe we should wear some disguise on the website."

"How about a picture in our Halloween costumes?" Emma suggested.

"Good idea, Emma," Kim agreed.

"We could take the picture at the school Halloween party. Is everyone here planning on going?" Emma inquired.

"If you haven't decided to go, think seriously about it. I'm on the planning committee and it's going to be the best party ever. A couple of mysteries will evolve for teams to solve. Maybe by the end the whole school will be interested in being part of the Kimsara Detective Agency." RT ended his plea by passing out small flyers advertising the party.

Kim and I decided on the ride home we definitely were celebrating Halloween at school. We wanted to go in complimentary costumes. From the bus we bee-lined to our costume options meeting Mom when we entered the house.

"Mrs. C. we've decided to go to the school Halloween Party."

"But we have a problem, Mom. We'd like to go as a team. Kim would really like to wear one of the gowns and I would like to be a Christmas tree."

"The gowns in the trunk are all summer, princess like," Mom admitted.

"Right, Mrs. C. I could wear the elf costume but ..."

"Kim's never dressed in a long gown whereas I have done it many times and would rather not."

"That's no problem." Mom pulled out her phone while asking, "Could you two please take the dogs for a quick walk before dinner?"

We agreed. Upon our return Mom announced, "We're going for a ride. Kim, your mother knows about it and agreed you can stay for dinner."

"Where are we going, Mrs. C.?"

"You'll see. Get in the car."

Mom got an unsettling update on the search for the dog thieves as she drove to Judith's house. After introductions we were led to a closet to view more costume possibilities. Mom opened a bag of gowns and pulled out a small red one holding it up in front of Kim. "I think this will fit you. Try it on."

"Okay, Mrs. C." Kim quickly slipped it on.

"Perfect fit, Kim," I declared. My mother and Judith stood by with accessories.

"Add this apron and wire rimmed glasses and you can be Mrs. Claus," posed Judith.

Mom suggested, "With these wings you can be a Christmas angel or without them a partygoer or caroler."

"Not, Mrs. Claus," we agreed. We took the wings leaving the final decision for later.

Chapter Forty-One

When we got settled back home the doorbell rang as simultaneously the door opened. "Hi, Sis," called my newly accepted brother, Jerry. He entered the kitchen followed by a petite blonde. "Amy needed a lift home. Can we stay for dinner before I take her home?"

"Of course," Dad answered. "You know your mother can always stretch dinner for a few more. Your timing is perfect. Join us at the table."

"Grab some muffins from the freezer first," Mom requested.

Jerry turned back to the mud room. He returned with bag of muffins which Mom opened placing the muffins on a pie tin before setting it on top of the wood burning stove that heated the house.

We sat down. After a brief blessing, taco fixings were passed. I introduced Kim. Jerry introduced Amy. He had told Amy about me as they drove.

"I live up the street about a mile and go to the same college as Jerry. My mom is a vet," Amy told me. A dog nuzzled her leg. "In fact, Jerry got Mitzy from her." Amy petted the dog then noticed the second dog.

"Wait a minute, you're not Mitzy."

"How did you know? They look so much alike," I noted.

"They do. But the dog I am petting has a microchip and I know Mitzy doesn't."

"A microchip?" I wondered.

"Yes, Mom usually puts one in the dogs she gives away. She charges $50 for the chip but is willing to refund the money if the dog gets neutered. I wonder if this is one of Mitzy's litter mates. I think there were six pups in the litter that mysteriously appeared on our porch. Was it three years ago?"

"Four," corrected Jerry. "Mitzy's four. Aren't you, girl?" He petted his beloved dog.

"How did this other dog get here?" Amy inquired.

"Long story," I admitted.

Mom gave Amy a brief summary.

"Sara, is Max the dog you took to Gina's baby shower?"

"Yes, why?"

"I assumed it was Mitzy though I noticed the dog acted differently."

"How so?" prodded Mom. "Max wasn't a problem, was he?"

"Oh, no. The dog was a delightful addition. The baby loved him. Sara, Max acted like you two had been together all your lives."

Chapter Forty-Two

"That's why it will be hard if his owner is ever found," hinted Jerry as if hoping to stop what he knew would come next.

"We could take the dog with today when Jerry drops me at home. My mom could read the microchip to find the owners," Amy offered.

"Do we have to?" I moaned, my high spirits totally deflating. Kim squeezed my hand in support.

"Yes, it's not fair to the owners," Dad cautioned. "You've grown attached to Max in the few weeks you've known him. Imagine how the people who had him for years feel."

"We don't have to do it today," Jerry bargained.

"It's not going to be any easier tomorrow. Please take him today," I pleaded grateful for Kim's supportive presence.

"Sara, that's a good idea. If you're lucky the owners gave up on finding him and have replaced him. They might be happy to know Max has found a new home. So don't get so down about this," advised Amy.

Max tried climbing into my lap, jolting the table and scattering some taco remains. As everyone laughed, I slipped from the chair, hugging my dog while assuring him,

"Max, you're mine. However, we need to let your former owners know that. Right, Amy?"

"Right."

I didn't get the usual warnings that I shouldn't get my hopes up, which surprised me.

"GTP time," announced Jerry walking to the wood stove, a potholder in his hand.

"GTP? Don't you mean, PTP?" clarified Amy. "What's on now?"

"No, he does mean GTP, green tomato pecan muffins," I explained as I held out the empty taco plate for Jerry. He slid the warm muffins on and offered the plate to Amy who looked apprehensive.

"Take one," Jerry insisted. "If you don't like it I'll happily finish it."

As the muffins were enjoyed, Mom began clearing the table. She excused Jerry and Amy from dishes. Kim went home. Jerry leashed Max who willing followed him but hesitated getting in the car. When I signaled from the door, "It's okay, Max. Go with Jerry," he jumped in.

"It'll be okay," Dad assured me while handing me a dish to dry.

A half hour later Max burst into the house followed by Jerry who waved a business card in his hand. "Max's owner has been found," he declared.

"Do they want him back?" pleaded I as I glared at him.

"I don't know but here's the information," Jerry said while handing me the business card with a name and phone number written on the back. "You can call them and find out. I gotta go."

He hugged our mother while thanking her for dinner. Our father walked with him outside.

Chapter Forty-Three

I handed the card to Mom who wondered, "Do you want me to call them?"

After a pause, I took back the card, pulled out my cell phone but paused when Mom mused, "It's late why don't you wait until tomorrow to call?"

A weak, "Okay," was all I could muster as I put my phone and the card away. Max was mine, if only for another day. I called Kim to commiserate.

The next day with the loss of Max looming, I avoided unnecessary conversation. At lunch Abdi approached the table followed by a beautiful girl who sat down next to Kim. She looked shy and scared. Her face peeked from behind her purple paisley headscarf.

"This is my cousin, Isad," Abdi announced. With pride at mastering our difference Abdi made correct introductions "Isad, this is Sara; and this is Kim. The guy joining us is RT. RT, this is Isad."

"I know Isad. She's in my class," he acknowledged while settling at the table.

Isad scowled, inquiring, "Aren't, you Dick?"

"That was the name I used as a kid. Now I prefer RT."

"Isad, you usually sit with the girls. I hope you don't mind me sitting next to you," noted RT.

"RT, if she did, she would let you know," Abdi assured him, proud of his shy cousin's determination to always speak the truth.

As everyone was finishing lunch I offered worn words that echoed from my past, "Isad, to what do we owe the pleasure of your company?"

After a few minutes of silence, as most left the table, Abdi spoke, "Tell her, Isad."

"My mother is out of town. She lets me use her tablet at home. Since she didn't need it, I brought it to school. I was using it at the library. When I got up to get a book, someone took it." Isad tried holding back my tears.

"Have you told anyone?" urged Kim.

Isad shook her head. She hadn't.

"She didn't even tell the media lady because she was ashamed she had lost it," confided Abdi. "The media lady's already gone. Today she is only here in the morning."

I abruptly left the group, returning with the principal as the bell announced the end of lunch. Abdi and Kim got up to go to class. The principal would help find the tablet. I checked, "Isad are you comfortable with me leaving you?"

"No, please stay. Abdi said that you are a good detective."

Chapter Forty-Four

The principal echoed, "Yes, please stay. I'll write you an excuse when we're done. Let's go to the media room. What time were you there Isad?"

"I do not know. I do not have a watch and the clock on the wall is broken, I think," she observed while pointing to a clock set on 6 o'clock.

"Isad, what period did you come here?" I prodded.

"Third period, after science I have a study hall."

"At the beginning or end of the period."

"The beginning."

"Principal Jones, that would be a little after 9:45."

"Thanks, Sara." The principal who had been working at the computer announced, "I have the footage with Isad in the library."

We all watched as Isad got up and a hand reached for the tablet. The hand and jacket sleeve were the only part of the person visible. "That's Herman Montale's jacket," I proclaimed with confidence. "He tried to grab my phone wearing that same jacket."

The principal called the secretary asking where Herman was. She knew exactly because she had seen him go into the nurse's office. "Please tell the nurse not to let him leave her office for any reason," ordered the principal.

We walked to the nurse's office. Herman shrank a little when he saw Isad. The principal ordered him to stand up, turn and raise his right hand. "Perfect match, right girls?" the principal announced.

"Yes, ma'am."

Isad demanded, "Where is my tablet?" A picture from the security tape was shown to Herman who quietly confessed.

"In my locker. I didn't know it was anyone's. I thought it was the one I had lost."

"To your locker, boy," demanded the principal as she took out a pad of paper from her blazer pocket. She wrote excuses for Isad and me as Herman pulled out the tablet.

"I'm sorry, I didn't..."

"Cut it," she quipped. "Isad, is this your tablet?" She handed it to her.

Isad powered it up, entered her pass word and saw a picture of her grandmother. "Yes, Principal Jones, it is mine. Thank you."

Herman sputtered excuses which were ignored. "You, girls, off to class," she admonished while giving us our excuses. We thanked her, turned and snickered as we noticed we had each other's excuse. We traded.

Before we split for different wings of the building, Isad stopped and hugged me. In hugging her back I pushed Isad's scarf off her head. I stood back in horror exclaiming. "I'm so sorry."

Isad smiled. "No biggie. I wear it because I am proud of my tradition and that way I don't have to fuss with my hair." As we parted she resettled her scarf.

I savored Isad's triumph. I told Kim about it on the bus home in such detail it took the whole trip. When we got off the bus Kim hugged me and wished me luck. It took a moment for me to remember why I needed luck. Then with dread, I shuffled home.

Chapter Forty-Five

Once inside the house I realized I was the only one home. I let both dogs outside for a run and dialed the number on the card for Oscar Austin. A woman answered.

"Are you missing a dog, possibly a four-year-old chow-husky mix?"

In response, "Oscar, the phone," was sharply growled as the phone banged down. In the background Oscar was being dressed down for not taking care of the dog.

A weak but deep, "Hello," was followed with silence.

"Oscar Austin?" I repeated, "Are you missing a dog, possibly a four-year-old chow-husky?"

"Yes, how did you find us?"

"Through the dog's microchip."

Then he yelled away from the phone, "Blanche, did you get Max microchipped?" Some unexpected cursing in the background indicated she had. He returned to the phone, "I'm sorry if the dog has given you trouble."

"No trouble at all. He gets along great with our dog."

"Since Max has been missing for almost three weeks, we gave up on ever seeing him again."

"So, you don't want him back?" I surmised trying to sound calm while bursting with hope-filled joy.

"It's really our son's dog. You should talk to him." He called, "Billy, pick up the phone and talk to this lady who found your dog."

I heard a new voice, a young one, saying, "Okay, Dad, I got the phone."

Before hanging up, Oscar Austin added, "Lady, I don't care if I never see that mutt again. But like I said, it's the kid's dog so you settle things with him."

Then Billy asked, "Where did you find my dog?"

"He found us."

"Where do you live?"

"Whistlestop."

"Where's that?"

"Near St. Cloud. Where do you live?"

"Hopkins, near Minneapolis."

"How did your dog get way out here?" pondered Sara.

He paused. Then in a barely audible voice the boy confessed, "I tried to sell my dog."

"You what?" I exclaimed.

"Listen, my mom didn't want the dog. She wanted my dad to take it to the country and shoot it. He offered to take it to the country and just let it go.

"I knew there were some guys picking up dogs. My buddy and I saw them put a dog in their van while we were walking Max. When I asked what they did with the dogs they claimed to be dog catchers who found good homes for strays. I told them I couldn't keep my dog and made up some story about my mom being sick and we needed money for medicine. I offered to sell them my dog. No deal but I decided giving the dog to them was better than having my dad shoot him. So I don't know how the dog got to your place."

"Billy, what color was the van?"

"Gray."

"Did it have any signs on the doors?"

"No. At school several kids had their dogs had run away that week. I figured those guys were stealing our dogs but I was too embarrassed to admit I gave Max to them. I told my parents that Max had gotten off the leash and ran away."

"Does that mean you don't want Max back?"

"He's better off anywhere but here."

"I will keep him then and he will have a wonderful life. Thank you."

"You promise you'll keep my secret of giving him to the thieves."

"I promise," I agreed while ending the call. Bubbling over with joy I hugged Mom as she walked through the door. Then I swung around exclaiming, "Max is mine. They don't want him back. He is mine." I sat on the floor holding my hands out, welcoming Max into my arms. The dog flopped down on me.

Mom allowed us a moment of bliss before asking, "Sara, did you want to discuss your composition?"

"Yes, but not tonight. I have some Math that's due tomorrow to finish. I'll email you what I've written."

Chapter Forty-Six

Before going to bed I bounced downstairs with my dog to announce, "I got a text from Billy, Max's former owner. He suggested we change the information on Max's microchip."

"Your mother already did that. She just got off the phone with Doc Bear. He's all yours, Honey," Dad announced.

I texted the news on my way up and was surprised that my phone rang as I entered my room.

"Hi, Sara, this is Billy. Thanks for getting the microchip changed."

I answered cautiously, "You're welcome," I wondered why he hadn't just texted the thanks.

"Why did you want to know the color of the van?"

"Because we believe a grey van is stealing dogs in our neighborhood. Why?"

"I saw the van yesterday and then found out my friend's dog is missing."

"Was this the first time you saw the van since it took Max?"

"No, I see it often. I think it belongs to someone in the trailer park."

"Has your friend gone to the police about the missing dog?"

"He called to see if someone had found his dog. No one had. They had many reports of runaway dogs that day but none of found dogs."

"The thieves may be the same ones we're investigating. We finally persuaded the police to look for the thieves. At first they couldn't be bothered."

"How did you get them to care?"

"We collected the names and dates for all the missing dogs. We also gathered information on dates the van was seen in our area. Several kids had been suspicious of it and so kept journals on when they saw it. There was enough of a match to see possible patterns. Right now about twenty of us let the police know when we see the van."

"Can't they just take the license plate down and go to the owner's house?"

"It's a stolen van. You could probably do the same thing with your friends. The van hasn't been seen in our area recently. So maybe it is concentrating on your area. We share our findings on our website: Kimsara.com. The van was originally white so we wouldn't be surprised if they repaint it again."

Hearing someone yelling in the background to get off the phone I wasn't surprised when Billy said, "Got to go. Bye."

"Text me," I urged.

"Can't. I borrowed my mom's phone to text you. Bye."

The next day a text from Billy surprised me. "Borrowed BFF phone. Van painted black. C photo."

I recognized the bumper sticker and passed the information on to the police. Instead of posting it to the Kimsara website, I tweeted everyone about it. That night Billy emailed me pictures of the van he had gotten from friends. One of the pictures showed the windows open and revealed the faces of the men. These were emailed to the police and Kimsara crew.

Chapter Forty-Seven

The next couple of days were a whirlwind of Halloween preparation. The night of the party Kim borrowed my fanciest shoes while I got my birthmother's brown Uggs. Dad had agreed to drive us to school. After a quick bowl of soup we donned our costumes. We thought we were set until Dad suggested we sit down. We couldn't. After moving some ornaments and redoing Kim's dress bow, we were able to sit comfortably. We had heard about scavenger hunts at previous parties so filled our purses with quality junk before getting in the car.

"Are you sure the party's at school?" Dad questioned, pulling up to a dark building with just a dozen cars in the parking lot.

"We're supposed to enter through the gym door. See the lights are on in the gym," Kim pointed out.

"Thanks, Mr. C. for the ride," Kim called out while carefully exiting the car.

Dad reminded us, "Kim, if for some reason your brother isn't able to pick you up at the end of the party, call me."

"Will do, Mr. C."

"Dad, have fun at The Whistlestop," I urged joining Kim. When we opened the gym doors, I turned around and waved good-bye to my dad.

"Kim, did you see that black van in the parking lot?" I groaned.

"It can't be."

As much as I wished it wasn't, I couldn't deny what I saw. Seeing RT approaching with concern prepared me for his news. "The police have been called about the van. Back up should be arriving soon."

"Backup?" questioned Kim.

"Yes, two from the police department had volunteered to chaperone tonight." A woman dressed in pajamas wheeled her chair over and joined us. RT made introductions. "Officer Lee, meet Sara and Kim."

"Tonight it's Lee, unless you want to be called Dick Tracy."

"So you know about the van in the parking lot," I sighed. "Is that why you're here?"

"I'm here because RT invited me. The van being here is not totally unexpected. Sara, when you emailed me about the van being seen in Hopkins, we contacted the police there. They had just begun making some connections on random crimes. They now suspect a criminal ring might be connected to your dog thieves."

Kim's stuttered, "Are they dangerous?"

I looked at Officer Lee whose face confirmed my suspicions.

"It would be foolish not to consider them dangerous. That's why tonight I want to meet with everyone connected with the Kimsara investigation."

Police sirens were heard in the distance. Van tires screeched. The van flashed out of the parking lot. Officer Lee seemed relieved. We would be safe for tonight.

Others joined us and watched as the police stopped the van. Emma, dressed as a birdwatcher, shared her binoculars. Our collective sigh of relieve was premature. A half dozen underage kids exited the van busted for smoking and drinking, not for stealing dogs.

County and city police continued to patrol the area in case the thieves' van appeared. In addition William Tracy's security firm at the request of his son, had fitted with school with a temporary edition of the security system he had hope to sell to the school.

Chapter Forty-Eight

At seven the school bell rang to officially begin the festivities. The outside doors were locked. RT, microphone in hand, announced, "Welcome. Let the party begin. Please find a partner for the grand march and line up behind Cleo and me."

The lights were dimming. The students lined up behind the ringmaster and clown. Chatter diminished as three different tracks of Halloween music began pulsing from different sections of the gym. The grand march started with each couple passing the camera under a canopy. Officer Lee's laptop displayed its video. She had agreed to pick the finalists for the best costumes so kept a tally of the ones she wanted to revisit. Halfway through the march, I saw Officer Lee's security screen surface as we joined the march. We could see that someone was trying to enter the school. William Tracy texted that a passing squad car had observed and questioned the kids who were trying to crash the party.

The grand march ended at the haunted house with its exotic assortment of sounds, smells, screams and in-your-face objects to spook us. Upon exiting we found the expected scavenger hunt list on the first table not far from the food and prize table. As the we snacked we tried to solve riddles and find the objects requested.

The Halloween music morphed into danceable music. One of the cheerleaders took the microphone and invited everyone to spread out in the gym. She taught us a simple line dance to the Addams Family theme song. That was followed by the circle dance mixer everyone had learned in their first sixth grade gym class. I easily picked it up.

Suddenly everyone connected with Kimsara was urged to gather by the bleachers for a group photo while the dancing continued. After the picture, Officer Lee spoke, "Thank you for all you have done to identify the dog thieves. They know people in this school are on to them. Keep your eyes open. Sorry the black van in the parking lot wasn't the dog thieves. Watch out for each other and keep us in the loop. Do not approach them or their vehicle for any reason." We all agreed to comply.

Chapter Forty-Nine

A drum roll stopped all the dancing. Officer Lee rolled to the mike, "After we announce the winners of the costume contest, the other prizes will be awarded.

The winners of the costume contest will receive a gift certificate to one of the local stores. The winners are..." As she paused the room quieted. Kim expected me to win, though for the first time she felt she might have a chance. From never getting a compliment on her past costumes she gloried in all she had received that night. Several categories of winners had been called when Kim's heart skipped a beat. "For most elegant costume, the winner is the Christmas caroler, Kim Porter."

I hugged Kim who wiped away her tears of joy. I knew winning was important to her. I realized I also had wanted to win. Then I heard, "The winner for most original costume is our Christmas tree, Sara Cowley."

I was delighted.

After prizes were awarded, we helped those taking down the remains of the haunted house. The cafeteria began looking like itself.

At ten o'clock, parents were allowed in the gym. Some helped with the final clean up. The kids who saw their rides in the parking lot left. Many wondered why three police cars were in the parking lot but figured they were just being proactive. Some Halloween pranks in the past had been quite destructive.

Just as I was about to call my father for a ride, Kim pointed out, "There's my brother. This was the best party ever."

"For me too," I agreed as I got into the backseat.

"Sorry, I'm late. A police chase in town slowed traffic," Aaron Porter reported. "A black van had three police cars after it going about 100 miles an hour."

"Did they get it?" I hoped.

"Listen," Aaron urged as he turned up the radio.

"A police chase through Whistlestop ended when the van drove off Hwy 10 and into some bushes. The van has been abandoned. Police dogs are searching the area. People in the east end of Whistlestop are urged to lock your doors and alert the police of any suspicious activity." The radio went on to the weather forecast.

"Glad we live on the northwest end of town," Kim confessed.

The radio again became our focus. "This just in: A white pickup truck was stolen at gun point from the Whistlestop park and ride. It had no license plates just a temporary sticker on the cab window. Anyone seeing this truck should call police immediately."

The ride continued in silence. While usually Kim and I ran back and forth to each other's house, Aaron insisted on driving me to the door. He waited until I unlocked the door and let the dogs out for a quick break. When I was behind locked doors he took his sister home.

Chapter Fifty

I was asleep by the time my parents got home. I left my most original costume certificate on the table for them to see. In the morning I summarized the highlights of the party. I totally forgot about the van sighting and police chase until I got to school. As Kim and I walked into school, still sharing exciting details of the party, Paul, RT and Abdi approached, each holding a copy of the day's paper.

"Sara, Kim, did you see this?" Paul extended the newspaper. The headline read, "Capture of Dog Thieves Thwarted." Pictures of two men and the crashed black van were included.

I commented, "I wonder where they got the pictures of the guys."

"The article says they are from the Hopkins police department," Paul explained. "Keep the paper, I want to get to class early." He and Abdi left.

RT walked silently with us a few steps before saying, "Officer Lee was right. These guys are dangerous. The article says that students in Whistlestop and Hopkins have been helping in the investigation. At first I was disappointed the Kimsara Detective Agency wasn't given credit."

I felt faint and wilted onto a nearby bench.

RT questioned, "Sara, are you all right?"

"Flashback?" questioned Kim.

I shook my head. I had momentarily flashed back to the family car and the oncoming car about to crash into us. Kim sat down next to me, reached into my backpack and pulled out my water bottle. She put it in my shaking hands while telling RT, "She'll be okay by lunch. See you then." He left with more questions than answers.

"Breathe, Sara. You're safe. Should I get the nurse?"

I issued a feeble, "No." Then moaned, "Will the flashbacks ever stop?"

"You told me even your Dr. Phil didn't know that answer. That's probably why she taught you what to do about them. You haven't been having as many as when I first met you," Kim reminded me.

"Right. Today is November 1st. I survived the car crash that happened a long time ago. I will survive the problems I face today and thrive," I recited using Dr. Phil's words. My face relaxed as I closed my eyes. I purposely visualized the car approaching exploding into a rainbow of butterflies.

I stood up, got a hug from Kim and sighed, "Let's get to class."

Chapter Fifty-One

As I approached the table for lunch I heard Kim tell RT that I was feeling better. Andy Parta also approached needling Kim, "How come you weren't at the church party last night?"

Kim ignored the question, proposing her own. "I suppose you won the Bible quiz again?"

"Of course and I won the costume contest," he bragged.

"You did not," Herman Montale corrected. "We don't have a costume contest." The two boys moved on to another table.

"I'm glad, holy roller Andy didn't join us. The school party was far more fun than any at the church," Kim assessed.

As Abdi joined the table he asked, "Sara, did you read the article?"

"Yes, thanks." I returned the paper. "I'm glad they didn't give the Kimsara Detective Agency the credit it deserves."

"Sara, how can you say that?" Kim demanded.

RT explained, "We're safer that way. Two guys with guns are on the run because of us. We don't need them looking for us."

"But we should be looking out for them. They know where we go to school," Paul reminded everyone.

124

"The police have been driving by school a lot today. I hope they continue until the guys are caught," wished Abdi.

"I'm hoping they leave town and never come back," added Kim.

"RT, do you think we should put our group picture on the Kimsara website?"

We discussed the pros and cons as lunch progressed. We decided to get Officer Lee's opinion and follow her suggestion.

When I got home after school I saw the day's newspaper on the counter. The door opened and both of my parents entered, having returned from walking the dogs. I greeted them noting, "Dad, you're home early."

I recognized a familiar scenario as my parents looked at each other and the newspaper. When my birth - parents were giving off the same vibe they ended up prohibiting me from doing what I wanted to do. I decided to take the lead.

I pointed to the paper commenting, "Too bad they got away." Seeing my parents silently communicating I continued. "We thought the van was in the school parking lot before last night's party. The police were not surprised at that. Two officers were in the building. There was extra security at the doors. The van turned out to be a different one, just some underage kids."

"Sara, those guys are dangerous," Dad paternally noted.

"The police have made us aware of that. That's why they were at the party. They also had squad cars circling throughout the evening. They were able to chase them when they returned like the article says."

"Your detective agency has been key to the operation," Mom noted.

"Yet Kimsara is not mentioned in the article as a safety precaution," I explained. "We're hoping they see our neighborhood is not safe for them and they'll stay away from here."

"I hope you are right," Mom admitted.

Chapter Fifty-Two

That evening after supper the doorbell rang. Kim entered holding her red Halloween dress. Her mother accompanied her apologizing, "Patty, Kim stained the dress you so generously lent her." She showed her the stain while glaring at her daughter.

"Vickie, that stain was there when she got the dress."

"I wanted to show you the stain before I got the dress dry cleaned in case you had some trick for getting it out."

"Vickie, these are costumes. They don't get dry cleaned. If anything, they get washed on gentle. I was going to wash our costumes. I can throw Kim's in with them," Mom offered while taking it. The women sat down while tea brewed. We ran upstairs until the barking of the dogs made us look downstairs to see Jerry entering with a huge canvas bag.

"I got the beast," he declared, prompting us to check it out. He pulled from his bag the largest frozen turkey I had ever seen.

"When I saw it at the store I remembered that our family has to bring one of the Thanksgiving turkeys. So I called Dad and he suggested I buy it. Do you want me to put it in the freezer?"

126

"No, put it in the refrigerator. It will take a while to unthaw," noted Mom.

In shock Vickie winced. "Will it be okay for three weeks in the refrigerator?"

"Mrs. Porter, Mom will cook it as soon as it thaws," explained Jerry rearranging the refrigerator to fit it.

Mom continued, "We have a huge Thanksgiving get together. We gave up on a picture perfect turkey years ago. Now we cook it ahead of time, slice it and freeze the slices. Then we reheat them. No more delaying dinner for hours because a turkey is not done, or eating a dry turkey because it cooked too fast."

"Sounds practical. I've given up on the whole Thanksgiving dinner," Vickie admitted.

Kim grumbled, "We just have sandwiches on Thanksgiving."

"Kim, your Father is so into football it doesn't make sense to have the traditional meal." She changed the subject. "Kim, did Sara help you find your homework answer?"

"We're working on it, Mom. We need about ten more minutes," Kim noted while she and I bounded back upstairs. Dad walked Jerry out leaving Vickie and Mom alone.

We quickly found the information Kim needed and headed back downstairs.

"Thank you. We'll tell them tonight," I heard as we came down the steps.

As they left Kim said, "Thanks again, Mrs. C. for the costume."

Chapter Fifty-Three

Mom told me, "Kim's parents are going on a second honeymoon to Brazil. They leave a week before Christmas and will be gone fourteen days. I suggested Kim and Marcia could stay with us while they are gone. I figured you would be okay with that, right?"

I had pulled out my phone as I agreed, "That's great."

Mom put her hand over my phone. "Kim doesn't know yet so wait until she contacts you about it," Mom cautioned.

An hour later Kim texted me that they were spending Christmas with us. We negotiated being together at Thanksgiving as well.

School days flew by. The Kimsara Detective Agency was convinced we had driven the dog thieves out of our neighborhood.

The Sunday evening before Thanksgiving I went to the parish youth center and joined 38 others, including my parents to practice Christmas carols. I had always wanted to go Christmas caroling but never had the chance. I was surprised to receive an old hymnal and be told, "There are so many carols in here we use it. Some other songs are pasted inside the covers."

Jenny, the youth director and Pastor Molly, the pastoral associate, came in greeting everyone. Then Pastor Molly took her place at the piano. The first song was White Christmas which we found inside the cover of the hymnal. After that we sang through the carols in the order they appeared in the hymnal. I giggled when O Come All Ye Faithful was followed by Jingle Bells which had been taped in what had been a blank space left on the page.

People added harmony here and there. I love singing harmony. Sometimes on Sunday Mom and I harmonize on the hymns like I had done with my birthmother on those rare occasions we attended church and knew a song. I brushed off the echo of cruel words from a classmate about my parents being in hell because they didn't go to church all the time. Fortunately, his voice was fading.

Before leaving we were handed a schedule of caroling times. Pastor Molly dictated, "No one is expected to make all the dates. There's a schedule on the newsprint pad. Please sign up for the ones you are sure you can make. Please check with your family and make sure those dates are okay for everyone.

Mom who had slipped out of the room moments earlier returned pushing a cart with Christmas cookies and drinks. As the carolers ate, Jenny looking at the signup board announcing, "We have at least 6 people for each engagement. Anyone else can join at the last minute."

I raised my hand and asked, "Can we bring friends who do not go to our church?"

A "yes" boomed from all corners of the room. "Sara, as long as they can sing, they are welcome. Just make sure you take a book for them."

I took a second hymnal for Kim, in case she could join us for some caroling. I helped my mom clean up and then we headed home discussing how many times we planned to carol.

Chapter Fifty-Four

On Wednesday morning Kim suggested, "We could go skiing during Christmas break. The place we go to rents skis. Do you have skis?"

"I think my skis will still fit me, but I don't know where my ski pants are. I had packed them but didn't remember if they had been in my large or small suitcase. Since neither survived the accident, I would need to get some or perhaps I could borrow Mom's."

After school I checked with my mom, "Do you think I would fit into your ski pants?'

"Absolutely not," she declared.

"But I'm not that much smaller than you," I reasoned.

Mom laughed. "Size isn't the problem. I don't own a pair of ski pants. I don't ski. I take it you need a pair of ski pants."

"Kim wants to go skiing during Christmas vacation. Her church group has an outing planned. My pants got lost in the accident."

"Wait, I think there's an old pair of Jerry's in the closet." She rummaged inside the closet for a few minutes before emerging with black bib ski pants. "Here, try these on."

I slipped into them adjusting the straps as my cell phone rang. A quick conversation later, I told my mom, "Kim called. She wants me to pick up some things for the robotics team garage sale from Mrs. Cremer down the street. She's heading south for the winter tomorrow and won't be back until February."

"Do you want me to drive you there?"

"No, thanks. I'll give these pants a test drive. I'll also take the dogs for a walk."

"How will you carry her items with the dogs? Maybe you should just take one dog," Mom advised.

I noticed Jeremy's empty camping backpack in the closet. I pulled it out, hoisted it on my back saying, "This should work. I'll be back in a few minutes." I added boots, jacket and gloves to my ensemble before picking up the dogs' leashes. I immediately had two wagging partners.

When I rang Mrs. Cremer's doorbell no one answered. Thinking it might not be working, I pounded on the door. I turned to leave when the door opened and I heard, "Hello, you must be the friend Kimmy sent. Come in."

"Yes, I'm Sara. However, I have two dogs with me."

"Bring them in too." She then went to a corner of the room where a box sat on top of the coffee table. She was perplexed. "Are you able to carry this box and hold on to the dogs?"

I had taken off the backpack, explaining, "I planned to put your things in here."

"Oh, good."

The items fit nicely. As I walked to the door, Mrs. Cremer remembered, "I forgot one item."

She went into the kitchen and returned with a large nonstick frying pan. "I don't think this is going to fit."

I suggested, "Not in the backpack but I have an idea." I took off my coat and tucked the pan into my bib ski pants. I put my coat on over it and declared, "It fits. Thanks, Mrs. Cremer the robotics team really appreciates your donation."

Chapter Fifty-Five

A light dusting of snow fell as we headed home. The dogs pulled me like a sled. All of a sudden Max growled and headed off the road as a white pickup approached. The two men looked familiar. As I tried to figure out why, the truck slowed. The window opened to reveal a gun pointed at me. I froze. A shot fired. I fell. A car horn blared.

I opened my eyes. Our neighbor and vet, Dr. Bear was leaning over me talking into her cell phone. The two dogs were licking me. Sirens were heard in the distance. I tried to get up from the cold snow bank. My chest hurt. Dr. Bear examined me. She asked with a smile, "Sara, why are you wearing a frying pan?"

I answered, "Doesn't everyone wear a frying pan when they take their dogs for a walk?" My chest hurt. She helped my up.

Then she told the 911 operator that the gunshot had been deflected and she was taking me home. Despite the operator's objections, she escorted me to her car. I told the dogs to go home as she drove the quarter mile to our home.

The dogs beat us there. They barked at the sound of the distance ambulance. It followed us into the driveway, turning off its siren and ending the barking. Mom opened the door, panic registering on her face. The ambulance driver was helping me out of the car.

Dr. Bear instructed, "Take her in the house. Patty, there's been an accident. The EMT's might as well examine her in the warm house."

My boots, jacket and snow pants were removed. The nonstick frying pan was held up so everyone could see the big dent caused by the bullet. "Are you having any trouble breathing?" an EMT inquired.

I answered, "My ribs hurt when I breathe. Did that frying pan stop the bullet?"

"That it did, a bullet aimed straight at your heart. You were lucky," the EMT exclaimed.

Mom considered, "Should I take her to the emergency room?"

"Only if she gets light headed or has difficulty breathing beyond her ribs being sore. She might find it easier sleeping in a recliner until her ribs heal. You might want to touch base with your doctor tomorrow," the EMT suggested. As they left Sheriff Tim Nixon approached the door.

Mom invited him in. I slowly and carefully sat up, entreating, "Sheriff, did you get the guys?"

"Yes, thanks to Dr. Bear's call and two squad cars being in the area. They are now behind bars. You must be Sara of the famous Kimsara Detective Agency."

I blushed.

Dad walked into the house with Kim at his side.

I pointed and told the sheriff, "And that's Kim."

"Sara, what happened?" Kim questioned.

The sheriff added, "Yes, please explain. I need your statement about what happened."

I began, "Kim, you and Mrs. Cremer saved my life." I painfully reached for the nonstick frying pan on the end table and held it up. Then I retold the story.

As the sheriff got up to leave he asked to take the frying pan for evidence.

Dad invited him to stay and share the soup bubbling on the stove. The sheriff declined the offer.

Chapter Fifty-Six

Kim stayed for supper. She kept on apologizing for having me pick up Mrs. Cremer's donations. She changed her focus. "Sara, is this a proof that everything happens for a reason?"

"No, everything does not happen for a reason!" I insisted.

"So you were just lucky. It was pure luck," Kim chided. Mom and Dad had heard us argue this point before. They sat back to observe.

I outlined my argument. "Kim, you asked me to pick up the donations. I could have said yes or no. You also proposed we go skiing over Christmas vacation so I was trying on Jerry's old ski pants. I could have left them on or taken them off before going over to Mrs. Cremer's. I also could have left the frying pan or carried it in my hands. I had many options that would have changed the situation."

"Would you accept that you were inspired to make the choices you made?" Kim countered.

I thought about it, admitting, "Yes, and I'm grateful for the way things worked out, except for the sore ribs. Though I will admit sore ribs are better than a bullet in my heart."

Then I changed the subject, "The thieves got caught. That's the important thing." I got up and put my

134

dishes in the sink. Everyone else followed. Kim waved goodbye and went home.

"I'm tired. I'm going to bed," I announced.

Mom prompted, "Do you want to sleep on the recliner?"

"I don't think so," I decided while slowly mounting the stairs.

Mom took a quilt from the linen closet. "If you change your mind, here's a quilt you can use." She placed it on the recliner.

The effort it took to get ready for bed surprised me. I put my head on my pillow and found breathing was harder in that position. I gathered all the pillows in the room and found laying on the pile made breathing easier. I immediately fell asleep.

After a few hours of sleep I awoke in pain. I took some ibuprofen and decided to try sleeping in the recliner. I headed downstair and smiled when I saw Max already at the foot of the recliner. Gingerly I settled in and fell asleep.

I awoke to the muffled sounds of parents milling around.

"Sorry, Dear," Dad apologized, "we were trying to be quiet enough not to wake you. Did you sleep all right?"

I yawned, shook my head and began to stretch. Then painfully I stopped.

Mom suggested, "Why don't you stay home from school today? Until we get you to the doctor you won't be able to take pain medication to school."

"I'll think about it," I agreed as I headed upstairs to get dressed for school. Fortunately I got an earlier than usual start.

When I finally returned downstairs in my butterfly shirt my parents knew I was going to school. Mom had made me a bowl of oatmeal thick with raisins and chocolate chips which I ate with relish.

"Do you want me to drive you to school?" Dad offered.

"That'll make you late for work," I reminded him.

"Right. I'm off," he a acknowledged, kissing Mom before leaving.

"I could drive you," Mom offered.

135

"Only if I miss the bus," I conceded while putting on my coat.

"If the pain gets too bad, call me," Mom insisted.

"Will do. Bye." I agreed moving as fast as I could to the bus stop, arriving just in time. I entered the bus to applause. I blushed and sat down next to Kim who was already there.

Chapter Fifty-Seven

The bus driver, two seats ahead, said, "Your partner told us what had happened. Congratulations on finally catching those dog thieves."

Those around me clamored for more details. I was tired and sore. Kim happily supplied the details.

I found my pain a distraction and wondered if going to school had been a good idea. Just before lunch there was an announcement.

The principal introduced Sheriff Tim Nixon who reported, "As many of you know thanks to the efforts of students in this school some dog thieves are now behind bars. Not naming this school or the detective agency operating out of it is being done on purpose. I am asking each one of you who posted any message on social media linking any individual or group from this school to the thieves to remove it.

"While we have two in custody we have reason to believe they had accomplices. One student nearly lost her life because of the investigation. We want all of you to be safe. Until we have assurances that they can't make bail and all aspects of the case are tied up, for your own safety, wait. Once it is safe I'll be back and we'll let the whole world know what you did.

"Two students have approached TV stations and offered to give details on the air. When the station approached us to verify their credibility we explained the situation. They will not be calling you back. They will be here to interview you on the day we make your deeds known. Until then be safe."

I dropped my plans to go home at lunch. Instead I gathered with the Kimsara regulars during lunch. No one would admit they had contacted a TV station.

Isad walked passed the table. People were moving together to make room for her. She stopped them. "No, your table is full. I just wanted to say I heard Herman Montale bragging that he was going to be on TV and thought you might like to know."

RT commented, "Leave it to a thief to take credit, false credit, for catching other thieves."

"Thanks, Isad," I responded trying to inflect energy into my words.

Kim cautioned, "Sara, do you think you should go home?" as she slipped ibuprofen into my hand under the table.

"I'm not sure." I added, "Thanks," when I realized what my hand held.

Abdi distracted the group by pointing out, "Isn't that Conner wheeling over here?"

Chapter Fifty-Eight

Everyone watched Conner maneuver his wheel chair toward us making it easy for me at the opposite end of the table to pop two pills into my mouth. Conner continued past the table and stopped next to me inquiring, "Are you okay?"

"Just a little sore," I admitted. "But I can't complain. Conner, you're sore everyday."

"Sore, but living," he retorted. "Dead people never feel sore."

I chuckled, winced and recognized, "Then I'm grateful to feel sore. Thanks for the pep talk, Conner."

"I have a question. Everyone at this table is part of your detective agency, right?" Conner checked.

I looked around before saying, "Yes, most of us are here."

"Is dragon lady with you?"

"Dragon lady?" Kim questioned.

"I know I shouldn't call her that but I never remember her name. She's by the door over there, the one in the red headscarf."

"That's Bennu," Abdi confirmed. "She definitely is not part of the Kimsara Detective Agency. Why do you want to know?"

"She acts like I'm deaf. She stood right in front of me while telling someone about going on TV to report more details about the dog thieves. I thought you should know."

"Thanks, Conner," Kim said. "I can see why the sheriff made his announcement."

Conner continued,"Since it's the Kimsara Detective Agency, Kim and Sara could be targets even though all of us are involved. So why don't you put on your webpage that Kimsara stands for: Kids In Modern Schools: Aware, Responsible, Active; or Keeping Informed, Making Social Alliances, Reporting Anomalies."

"Conner, that's a great idea," RT praised with everyone at the table clearly agreeing. "Did you write those down, by any chance?"

"RT, you know I always write my ideas down." Conner ripped out a page of his ever present notebook and handed it to RT. During his Math period, RT posted the additions.

I made it through the rest of the day, glad it was a Friday.

I rested most of that weekend. Mom drove me on Sunday night to the Senior Center where the youth group was caroling. I refused to back out of my commitment. However, after two carols I admitted singing was too painful and returned home with Mom.

Very gradually my ribs healed.

Chapter Fifty-Nine

On the Wednesday before Thanksgiving, I returned to my former home in Elk River to help Gina set up. I retrieved the Thanksgiving decorations I had stored the year before. Together we decorated while Max entertained the baby.

"Sara, I really appreciate your help," Gina sighed as she eased into the couch. "How are you doing?"

"Doing?" I wondered. Then I realized what Gina was really asking. "Are you asking if I miss my family?"

Gina blushed.

"I do, but holidays always meant the whole family: aunts, uncles, cousins, everyone. When it was only our family, the four of us, things weren't that great. Mom and Dad fought a lot which made me nervous. When everyone else came over, I knew they wouldn't fight. I miss my family, but I don't miss the fighting."

Gina pointed to her baby, Jordan, sound asleep in his swing. Max gently butted the swing to keep it moving. "I better tuck him in bed. If you are all set for the night, I'll wish you a good night."

Grateful that my ribs had healed enough for me to sleep in a bed, I headed up to my old room. It looked too little-girly. Max seemed unfazed by the change in room. As I got ready he settled on the bed as usual. I climbed in next to him. After a quick text to Kim, I gave Max a hug and fell sound asleep.

Thanksgiving morning Uncle Vince's booming voice woke me up. "Breakfast is getting cold, Sara. How many pancakes do you want? Will seven do?"

As I hurriedly dressed I called back, "One." He made me three which I quickly devoured, leaving nothing for Max.

Gina wondered, "How was it sleeping in your old room?"

"Okay, though it doesn't feel like home anymore." I stacked my dishes in the dishwasher. "Do you need me right away? I'd like to go through my clothes and put the ones I don't want in a bag for Goodwill, if that's okay with you."

"That's fine. You'll do a better job than me," chuckled Uncle Vince as he bundled the baby in his snowsuit. "We're taking Max for a walk, unless you have some objections."

"No, he looks like he's ready." Max stood by the backdoor with his leash in his mouth. Vince hoisted Jordan in his backpack carrier, grabbed the leash and left.

I repeated, "Do you need my help for anything?"

"No, I plan to rest until the boys get back. We're set until eleven when people arrive."

I headed upstairs. Looking through my clothes, I was amazed I had grown so much since last year. Kim was smaller than me so I put the best rejects aside for her. If they were too small for her they would eventually fit her sister, Marcia.

I put the few items that still fit into a pile. I was missing a few key items, the items I had packed in my long-term suitcase. My father had told us to pack for two weeks but to put other clothes in a bigger, metal suitcase in case we liked where they were going and decided to stay for six months. If we decided to stay, we would send for the suitcases. I wondered what happened to those suitcases. They couldn't have been in the trunk of the rental car at the time of the accident.

After sorting my clothes, I went into my parents' bedroom. My father's clothes were gone, replaced by Vince and Gina's clothes. I found my mother's walk-in closet untouched. Did I want any of her clothes? I decided to have my new mom go through them with me to see if any should be put in the costume closet.

My brother's bedroom had been converted into the nursery. When Gina called to tell me they were moving in I told her that she should take Justin's clothes and toys for Baby Jordan.

Chapter Sixty

I heard a commotion and went downstairs just as my parents were entering with Kim and Marcia. I greeted them and helped put away coats. Max who was serving as a pillow for the baby looked up at the family. He welcomed my command to stay.

I took my friends to the dining room to set the tables. Four tables had been set up with ten chairs at each table. As we set out silverware, Marcia commented, "Wow, Sara, you have a big family."

"Everyone here won't be family. In fact Gina only expects thirty-eight people."

"Then why are we setting forty places?" Kim questioned.

I thought for a moment. "It's a tradition to set extra places in case of unexpected guests."

"Like us?" Marcia squeaked.

"No, you're part of the thirty-eight."

"Where's the kids' table?" Kim asked as two toddlers entered the room.

"We don't have one." I introduced three-year-old Sissy and four-year-old Randy. As he reached for a chocolate turkey, I picked him up adding, "We used to have a kids' table when I was a kid. Now the kids are put in between adults. Their parents sit at a different table with other people's kids."

When most of the guests had arrived I clapped my hands. The room got quiet. "Thanks everyone for coming."

144

Most were surprised at my words. I repeated my father's exact words ending with, "I'd like to introduce my friends, Kim and Marcia who are joining us today. They live next door to me now."

Fifteen-year-old Cousin Gary prodded, "Would you be Kim of the Kimsara Detective Agency?"

Marcia answered for her sister, "Yes, that's her and the Kimsara Detective Agency stopped the thieves from taking our dogs." Small conversations broke out, many had information on Kimsara because they had been following them on the internet.

In the kitchen a highly choreographed ritual heated the arriving food. Potatoes were mashed. Gravy was divided into the quart measuring cups. As food advanced to the table, people settled behind chairs. Toddlers were tucked among the teens and adults.

Cousin Gary tapped his glass with a knife proposing, "I'd like to say grace." No one objected. So he read the prayer he had prepared.

Then everyone responded, "Amen," sat down and began passing the food.

The doorbell rang and opened at the same time. "Sorry, we're late," my brother, Jerry called out. He entered the room with his girlfriend, Peaches, who held a small casserole in her gloved hands and set it on a table."

"Thanks," cheered Kim as she removed the cover. "This is my favorite vegetable dish." She dished some up for herself and for Marcia. The green bean casserole circulated from table to table and was empty by the time Peaches and Jerry settled at their places."

The table discussion was lively. Kim and Marcia were invited into it. By the end of the meal they acted like family. Several of the men cleared the dishes and the food. Some of the teens began washing dishes. Left overs were bagged and placed in the refrigerator or in coolers.

The little kids went to the living room to empty the big toy box reserved for large family celebrations. Max circulated cleaning hands, faces and clothes of missed crumbs.

Chapter Sixty-One

Tables were folded away. Chairs were moved to form a large circle. As everyone settled on them, Uncle Roger, the brother to both of my moms announced, "It's my turn to coordinate Christmas. Whoever wants Christmas Day here at 1 p.m. say, 'aye.'" Everyone responded.

"Any nays?" None were heard. "So we have place and time set."

Uncle Roger's wife, Aunt Shelley continued, "We have the family commitment to serve lunch at the homeless shelter on Christmas Eve. How many will be able to make it?" Looking around she continued, "So, everyone except Pearl, Stella and Pete are able to make it."

"It's the pits having to work holidays," moaned Pete.

"At least we have jobs," Cousin Stella reminded him.

Roger continued down the Christmas planning list, "Now, the harder part: gifts. Any suggestions?"

"What if we say the gifts can't cost more than a dollar or be something we already have? You know, regift," suggested Aunt Diane.

"White elephant gifts, strictly white elephant gifts; I'm for that," Grandma Jo agreed. After a lively discussion all seemed to favor re-gifting.

"What's a white elephant gift?" Cousin Gary asked.

Mom explained, "You look through your things and pick something to give away that someone else would enjoy."

"If you don't find anything, check with your parents. We all have plenty of extra stuff," encouraged Uncle Pete.

I felt honored as Aunt Linda admitted, "It worked so well at the baby shower. I'm glad we're doing it again."

"So let's draw names and everyone get one gift," suggested Roger as he reached for the box which containing everyone's name. I had put Kim and Marcia's name in the box earlier that day.

He walked around as everyone picked out a name, opening it so no one else saw. Then the names were collected for the next year.

I assured Kim and Marcia I had gifts for the two names they had drawn, no matter whose names they had gotten.

After the discussion many retired to the basement to watch football. Others tossed frisbees outside to each other and to Max. Some went for a walk. I took Kim and Marcia upstairs where we bagged all the clothes to take home for further consideration. After an evening snack of turkey sandwiches, we headed home.

On Saturday our neighbor Vickie came over to say, "The girls really had a great Thanksgiving. Thanks for all the leftovers you sent over. Since only Joe and I were home on Thanksgiving, we were happy with turkey sandwiches and TV. Then thanks to your leftovers, we had a real thanksgiving dinner on Friday. Joe actually sat at the table with the TV turned off. He even led grace. Having no kids home on Thanksgiving made Joe realize how much he treasured the kids and how much he was taking for granted. Thanks."

"Are you still going on that second honeymoon?" Mom checked.

"More so than ever. Will you still take Kim and Marcia?"

"Definitely."

"Thanks again, Patty. Got to go."

147

Chapter Sixty-Two

That afternoon I went next door. Kim and Marcia had gone through my hand-me-downs. They only rejected three items which we put in the Goodwill box. We decided to build a snow sculpture outside. Instead of the usual snowpeople, we would sculpt a Nativity set. Ten inches of new snow that week fueled our enthusiasm. Our creation would be near enough the road to be seen but far enough so the snow plows wouldn't cover it. A small hill adjoining both properties fit the bill. All week as we worked we made plans for our Christmas time together.

I had faithfully done my doctor recommended breathing exercises. I found breathing and talking easier. Confident I could carol and I tested it out one night. Kim joined me and the other the carolers at the St. Benedict's independent senior condos. As we sang, a distraught woman opened her door and motioned to Pastor Molly. After a brief conversation Pastor Molly gestured for Kim and me to join her and the woman who had come out. As we left the group I heard how amazing the group sounded and wondered why we had been summoned.

As we approached she opened her door and invited us in. We entered and took off our boots.

The woman called, "Here boy." A beautiful German shepherd came towards us.

148

"Where are my manners? I'm Mrs. Nelson." We shared our names and the usual chit chat ensued. Then Mrs. Nelson got to the heart of the matter. "What do you notice about the dog's coat?"

Immediately Kim observed, "It looks like this dog wore a service vest."

"I thought so too," agreed Mrs. Nelson.

"How did you get this dog?" I questioned.

"I was taking my daily walk. At 88, the daily walk is important; slow, but important. I saw some boys in the field across the street tormenting this dog. So I yelled as loud as I could for them to stop. I steadied myself against the mailbox and shook my cane in the air. They ran off and the dog came to me. He immediately walked on my left side. He stood in front of me when we came to an intersection. There was a car coming down the road. That made me think it was a trained helper dog."

"When did this happen?" I asked.

"Today. I can't keep the dog. Dogs aren't allowed in these buildings unless they weigh less than 20 pounds." In a teasing voice she added, "I think he weighs more than twenty pounds."

"Oh, just four or five times more," quipped Kim.

"Can you help me?" pleaded the woman.

"Yes, if nothing else, he can come home with me until we find the owner," I assured her. While I talked I dialed my phone. "Hello. Do you have any reports of a missing German Shepherd, possibly an assistance dog?"

"We're not sure where he came from but we found him when we were caroling. He won't answer any command to go home and he looks hungry. I'll be taking him to our place until we find the owner." I then gave my name, address and phone number.

"Do you have anything we could use for a leash, Mrs. Nelson?" I inquired.

She put her hands together bent her head a bit as if in prayer. One teardrop ran down her cheek as she turned and went to a drawer in the kitchen taking out a well worn leash. "This belonged to my Scotty. He was old and died shortly before I moved. I couldn't throw it out but had no idea what I would use it for until this minute. Please take this. Scotty would want the helper dog to have it."

"Thank you, it will help us get this dog home," I promised.

We said goodbye wishing each other the best holiday. Mrs. Nelson hugged us. She seemed happy but another tear was forming.

I remembered what I had heard about grieving taking a lifetime and its okay to cry. I felt a tinge of grief for my parents as I left leashed to the dog.

Chapter Sixty-Three

Once outside, panic struck because the carolers were no where to be seen. Before I could articulate our problem, we heard laughter coming from a house down the street followed by the exodus of the carolers. Pastor Molly approached us with two cups of hot cocoa.

"I figured you would be taking the dog home. Do you think you can find the owner?"

"No problem," I confidently reported.

"What will your parents say when you bring the dog home?"

"I'll find out when I get home."

"Okay. If you're comfortable taking the dog, ride with me in the parish van."

By then we had caught up with the rest of the carolers. Pastor Molly arranged for two carolers to change places in the vehicles.

At the next house the dog was noticed. A voice called out, "For the puppy," as a pail of water was shoved out the door. I led the dog to the bucket which he nearly emptied. Calling out a thank you we continued to the next house.

By eight o'clock the vans were loaded and approaching the teen center. The carolers sang the whole way. The dog howled through "Joy to the World," creating a chorus of laughter.   When we passed the center I remembered that the people who volunteered to drive also volunteered to take everyone home.

Pastor Molly dropped off the kids in town first. "How do you know where everyone lives?" asked Kim.

"It's part of my job," Pastor Molly reported as we pulled into my drive.

"I'll get off here," Kim announced. "My house is right next door."

We got out and waved to Pastor Molly.

We walked to where I could see Kim as she ran home with her carol book. I knew that Dad had come out and was watching.

He tried to be cool, "Hi, Sara. How was caroling?"

"Great," I exclaimed.

We walked into the house casually as if I always came home with a stray dog.

Finally I couldn't contain myself. "Dad, don't you see the dog?"

Mom joined us trying to contain a smile.

The guest dog immediately went to Max and Mitzy's dog bowls, emptying both. Max and Mitzy sniffed and smelled at the dog but didn't seem to mind empty bowls. Dad refilled the dishes. Neither of our dogs were hungry. All three moved to the living room and sprawled out over the dog mats as if they did this every night.

"Of course I see the dog, Pumpkin. I figured when the time was right you would tell us how he picked you up."

"Oh, Dad. Pastor Molly called you didn't she? What did she say?"

"Just that you had picked up a stray dog and would it be okay for you to bring it home," reported Mom. "Of course I agreed."

"A bit of déjà vu," Dad added.

"Déjà vu?"

"Yes, your brother Jerry must have brought a dozen stray dogs home. So why should his sister be any different," Dad acknowledged. The brother sister vocabulary rolled off his tongue with ease. We were family.

Chapter Sixty-Four

I told the whole story while Mom pulled out some left over pizza. I nibbled the pizza while my parents requested details. They agreed that it did look like it had worn a some kind of vest.

"What police department did you call?" Dad queried.

"Our Sherburne County Police Department."

"What county were you caroling in?"

"Oh, no, I called the wrong county," I admitted.

Dad, thinking ahead, passed me the phone book pointing to the correct phone number.

I called giving the same information as before but got a different response. I gave them our address, phone number and some basic directions on how to find us. I was ecstatic when I hung up.

"Rex, come." The dog responded to the command immediately. "Your owner is on the way to get you."

A half hour later a Sherburne County police car drove up to our house. The officer introduced Mrs. Boxer and helped her out of the car as Dad opened the door. The minute the door opened Rex bounded out and to the woman's side.

"Would you like to come in for something to eat or drink?" offered Mom.

"No, thank you," muttered the woman, slowly moving back toward the car. "Thank you for finding my dog. I don't know what happened to his vest, but that can be replaced.

Mom quickly slipped into the house and returned with a dog vest explaining, "Our dog, Mitzy dressed as a rescue dog one Halloween."

"For all of ten minutes," added Dad.

Rex allowed Mom to slip the vest on. A tear of joy fell as Mrs. Boxer hugged Mom and got into the car. "Thank you all," she said as the officer helped her with her seatbelt. Rex sat at attention next to her.

The next day, the principal called me to her office during math. I was confused and tried to think of what I had done to get called to the principal's office. My mood darkened as I saw the principal talking to the police officer who had picked up Rex.

"I need to get your statement on how you got the dog," established Officer Sally Minks.

"Why don't you use this conference room?" advised the principal as she opened the door to the room.

I again told the story to Officer Minks. I added, "The woman in the senior condo won't get in trouble. Will she?"

"I highly doubt it."

"Why was the owner of the dog in such a hurry to get home?"

"Mrs. Boxer can't see very well. Rex is her eyes. She was shopping at the mall when she was pushed down, she thinks by two men. We think the dog was drugged because she said the dog fell down too and seemed to be dragged away from her. She called Rex and got no response. They also got her purse which only contained ten dollars and some cents. She keeps her identification and checkbook in a pouch under her sweater.

"Someone saw what happened and called the police. A few people stuck around and gave a description of the men to the police. Someone even got the get away car's license. It was a stolen vehicle. Though we think we know who they are.

154

"Mrs. Boxer had been without her dog for two days."

"That's why the dog was so hungry. He emptied both of our dogs' dishes."

"And your dogs didn't get upset?"

"No, they're both real mellow and knew their dishes would be quickly refilled, which they were."

Chapter Sixty-Five

"Mrs. Boxer's daughter was staying with her to help out. If the dog hadn't been returned by the end of yesterday, Mrs. Boxer would have been placed in a nursing home by her daughter today. She is so grateful you stepped up to unite her with her dog," explained Officer Sally Minks.

"Mrs. Boxer wanted me to give you her phone number and address. She would like if you have time, for you to stop by to see her so she can thank you. She apologized for wanting to leave so quickly. She hadn't slept the last two days. Could you at least call her?"

"I'll do that. When I called the Sherburne County police station they didn't have any report of a missing dog. When I called Stearns County they had one. You're here from Sherburne. I'm confused."

"The dog was taken in Stearns County so they had the report. Mrs. Boxer lives in our county so we were closer to her and you."

"Why didn't you ask us to take the dog to Mrs. Boxer?"

"Mrs. Boxer was so desperate to get her dog back the police were afraid whatever dog you brought she would say it was hers. They didn't want her left with a dog who couldn't help her. So Stearns had us unite the pair in the

156

way we did. I would have waited to talked with you at your home tonight but your mother gave me permission to talk to you at school. I also cleared it with your principal."

She continued, "You live at that house where the hunter was found with his leg cut by a trap."

I admitted, "Yes, did you ever find out how the guy got the trap off?"

"No, the guy claims a bear took it off. That's not possible."

"Oh, I don't know about that." I thought for a microsecond about telling her about Bury Bear but decided against it.

"Have the FBI or Homeland Security contacted your family about the man?" she inquired.

"Not that I know of, why?"

"They requested the report but must not have found any reason to investigate. Do you still have that stray black dog who was at the scene?"

"Yes, we have Max. We found his owners through his microchip. They told us to keep him. He's actually our dog's brother. The dog thieves got him in Hopkins and he must have gotten loose here."

"And he's working out okay with the other dog?"

"Couldn't be better."

"Thanks again for your help. Now that the dog thieves are caught, you're closing your detective agency, right?"

"I don't think so. We haven't talked about it."

"Be careful, Sara. Be careful," the Officer advised as she left.

The lunchroom buzzed with questions about the police coming for me. I was glad the Kimsara Agency filled the whole table around me to hear the story of Rex. Abdi then pulled out his neon green notebook and wrote the date and the case of the missing assistance dog solved. He had become the official Agency chronicler.

Chapter Sixty-Six

That weekend Mom and Dad brought out the Christmas decorations. Since Kim and Marcia were going to be living with us for the holidays, they were invited over to help decorate. We stood overwhelmed by dozens of boxes of decorations. Kim and Marcia's family usually put up a Christmas tree but not much more. Since my home had been the extended family's gathering space people took turns decorating it. Every year it was different.

I pleaded, "Mom, where do we start? What goes where?"

"Start anywhere you like. Use whatever you find. The boxes contain years of decorating using different themes and color schemes. Please do not put everything out. We're going out shopping. You don't have to get all the decorating done today. We'll be back in a couple of hours."

We seriously sorted through our options creating color matched piles before deciding on purple, blue and silver for the living room and dining room. We used the red for the kitchen.

We were in the bedrooms adding a few festive touches here and there when my parents arrived home.

Mom exclaimed, "Girls, the house is elegant. Thank you."

That evening as we prepared dinner Dad checked, "Are you all set for Christmas, Sara?"

"Almost. I need to get to Gina's to get gifts for the family white elephant exchange."

"And what would that be?" Mom slipped in.

"A white elephant, of course," Dad quipped. "I'm leaving work early tomorrow to run some errands. I could pick you up from school, drop you off, run my errands and retrieve you. Would an hour be enough time?"

"That should work. Could Kim come with?"

"Just make sure she gets a note from one of her parents so I'm not stopped for kidnapping her," Dad insisted.

"Sara, let Gina know you'll be stopping by."

"I will. By the way I don't need a new phone. I know the two of you have been looking at them. Just in case you were thinking of getting me one, please don't. I don't want a new phone. I have my mom's phone. It's a little banged up but it works perfectly."

"What do you want for Christmas?" Mom inquired.

"A quiet home with no one fighting. No gift certificates. I hate them. I don't like shopping."

Chapter Sixty-Seven

After school the next day I rummaged through my birthmother's wallpapered, walk-in closet. I gave Kim a lunchbox sized jewelry box, reminding her, "You need a gift for Aunt Linda, right?"

"Yes, she wore the blue dress with the cameo earrings," Kim remembered.

"Yes, she loves cameos and the color blue. In this box you should find a cameo brooch or a blue windmill piece that Aunt Linda would like. I think Mom called it delft jewelry."

I opened the box surprised at the disarray inside it.

Kim systematically laid out all the jewelry on the floor in the hall while I looked for a red silk blouse that my mother wore for special occasions. I found it. As I slipped it on I asked "Kim, do you think my mom will like this blouse?"

"That red is really bright. Wow, I think any woman would like it."

"It's fancier than the blouses she wears." I pulled the cowl collar up so the sweeping pleats of the front were more visible. The tunic length looked more like a dress than a blouse on me.

"The color is wrong for you but I think would be great on your mom."

"I think so too. Did you find some jewelry that you would want to give Aunt Linda?"

"Would one of these work?" Kim had three one inch brooches: the face of a young woman on a deep blue background surrounded by seed pearls, a blue cameo angel surrounded by white gold filagree with tiny blue sapphires and blue windmill framed in silver and highlighted with one blue diamond. I was surprised I had remembered how my dad had described each piece.

"Any one of them would work. Mom kept what she called "serious" jewelry in that box. Bring all three." I thought my mom meant expensive but it would be months before I learned each of the three pieces was worth over five hundred dollars.

"Should I put one of them aside for Marcia to give to Gina?"

"No, Gina's gift should come from the fun jewelry box," I decided as I opened the doors on a four-foot jewelry armoire. "Someone has messed this all up. The necklaces aren't supposed to be in a heap on the bottom. Mom always put them on the hooks." I began properly hanging them.

Kim joined me, stopping when she found a necklace of smiling lady bugs. "I think this would be perfect for Gina."

"I agree." I rummaged through one of the drawers. "Here are the matching earrings and I think there are three bracelets." We found them.

"I'll straighten up the rest of the jewelry another day. We should wrap our gifts. Mom always kept little boxes in this big box," I remembered. Opening a large box I pulled out some small boxes that once held jewelry.

"Your Mom sure has a lot of jewelry."

"But she didn't wear very much. Most of it is from my dad's mother and grandmother."

As we gathered the right size boxes I noticed how the busy floral wallpaper distorted the walk-in closet. I saw my mother's robe hanging on a peg on the wall. I put it on smelling my mother's lilac scent, missing her deeply.

161

Feeling a little faint I steadied herself by grabbing the peg. I jumped because the wall behind it opened.

Kim gasped, "Did you know that secret space existed?"

"No." We peered in. In the secret space crammed a locked filing cabinet without much room for anything else. Two colorful pictures were on the wall.

Kim noted, "Is that a shopping bag behind the cabinet?"

"It looks like it." I reached back and noted, "There's something in it but there's not enough room between the cabinet and the wall to pull it out. It feels heavy."

"Try lifting it up to the top of the filing cabinet."

"That works," I beamed as I pulled it across the cabinet. The sound of a horn tooting signaled Dad's arrival.

"We gotta go. Let's take the bag with us. The jewelry boxes will fit in it. We can explore it at my house." I closed the door to the passage and tidied the closet. I took off my mother's robe, slipped the red blouse inside it and slipped it through the bag's handles as we hurried downstairs.

Chapter Sixty-Eight

I hastily thanked Gina as we rushed to the car. I set the bag inside then remembered, "Oops, I wanted to get something from the garage." The garage door opened as I approached it.

Gina poked her head out of the kitchen door saying, "Glad you didn't forget. I put the items you wanted in the shopping bag by the door."

"Thanks, Gina," I called as I swooped in, grabbed the bag and ran out. "See you on Christmas." The garage door shut behind me.

Dad inquired, "Did you girls find what you wanted?"

"Yes, Mr. C., more than we wanted. We just have to wrap them. We could probably do that tonight."

She looked for confirmation from me, but I stared in space while my mind raced. "Dad, did someone break into the house? Mom's jewelry was all messed up."

"Anything missing?"

"None of her gold chains were there but I thought she packed those."

Changing the subject Dad asked, "Do you girls have homework tonight?"

"Yes," we both groaned.

"Then you should tackle that when you get home and leave the gift wrapping for another time."

163

We agreed, separating when we arrived home.

The next day after school we pulled the bags from under my bed. We took the jewelry boxes to Mom's office. "Mom, do you have a minute?"

"Perfect timing, I'm ready for a break. What is it?"

"Mrs. C., which of these three brooches would be the right one to give to Sara's Aunt Linda." She opened the three boxes on the desk.

Mom's eyes widened. She gasped, "Sara, you know these are very expensive pieces of jewelry."

"Yes," I acknowledged."Are you saying I can't give them away?" When Mom remained speechless I continued, "Do I need to save them to pay for my college tuition?"

"No, your parents have taken care of that nicely. However, these are heirloom quality pieces. You might want them someday."

"My mom never wore them, did she?"

"I guess not."

"Her walk-in closet doesn't need them, does it?"

"Don't be silly, of course not."

"Mrs. C. they are so pretty."

"Mom, it's a shame no one sees them. I would like to give them to someone who might wear them. Which one would be the best one to give to Aunt Linda, or should Kim give her all three?

"One is more than enough. I think the windmill one would be best. She has so many cameos she might already have either of those."

"Can...may I give the angel cameo to Peaches, Mom? It's been hiding in the closet long enough. Can't you see her wearing this?" I urged winking puppy-dog-eyes.

"Yes, I can see her wearing it. Go ahead. I suppose you have plans for the third brooch. I hoped those plans don't include me. Cameo jewelry is not my style."

"May Kim give it to her mother for Christmas?"

"We were thinking I could wrap it up and slip it into her purse when she wasn't looking. Is it okay to give it to my mom?"

"Yes, Kim, but don't wrap it up. She'll just have to unwrap it when she goes through airport security." Mom rummaged through a drawer and pulled out a small pre-wrapped box. She opened it. "Kim, you can use this box and it'll be easier if she has to open it when she goes through security."

"Thanks, Mrs. C., it's so small it'll be easier to hide in her purse. Look, it fits perfectly."

Chapter Sixty-Nine

I pulled out another box from my bag. Opening it I appreciated Mom's comment, "That would be perfect for Gina."

"She's the one getting it," I affirmed with pride.

Mom put out her hand to stop me from pulling out another box, saying, "Sara, everything in that house is yours. You can do with it what you want. You can ask my opinion if you need it but you don't have to show me everything you want to give away. Just make sure you're not giving away Vince and Gina's things."

Mom then got up and pulled out her plastic tote of wrapping paper. "Here you can use this to wrap your gifts. Unless, you desperately need my help, go wrap your presents. I need to fix dinner."

Offering swift thanks, we rushed upstairs with the tote and wrapped the jewelry. Then I pulled out the cake pan I had taken from the garage. I lined it with red tissue paper and tucked in the blouse noting, "Mom's cake pan is beat up and the cover doesn't stay on. This will make a perfect box."

I pulled out a car cleaning kit still wrapped in plastic. "I got this for my dad last Christmas but couldn't find it to give him. So I gave him a card saying he would

166

get a car cleaning kit when I found where I hid it. I didn't find it before we left. I think Jerry would like it."

"I do too," Kim agreed.

We piled up the wrapped gifts then spilled the contents of the secret compartment bag on the bed. Several plastic grocery bags emerged. In one a box read: "NEW MOULTRIE Game Spy M-990i No Glow Infrared Digital Camera." I explained, "Mom got that for my dad during the summer. Then Dad bought his own and installed it just before Christmas. Mom got mad and talked about returning it."

"It's probably too late to do that," Kim advised.

"I don't have a present for my current dad. I think I'll wrap it and give it to him."

"Why not?" agreed Kim while I opened another bag taking out a package beautifully wrapped in violet and periwinkle paper. Ribbons in silver and purple cascaded from the top where a tiny silver angel announced the package was for me from Dad.

We stared in amazement. "Sara, open it."

"No, I'll wait until Christmas. Let see what's in the other bags."

"Maybe there's a key for the filing cabinets," Kim speculated.

No key appeared. We found an old tablet, my mom's day planner and a pouch containing some gold chains. I slipped them into my bottom drawer just before we were called down for dinner.

Mom offered, "I'd invited you stay for dinner, Kim but since your parents are leaving soon..."

"Thanks, but I want to be home for dinner. You're all coming over for dinner tomorrow night, right?"

"Yes, Kim, I couldn't persuade your mom to come here to eat. I did agree that we would clean up after dinner and stay until they leave for the airport. The travel agent's van is picking them up around eight for their midnight flight. We'll lock up the house and help you girls move in with us," Mom explained.

"My mom's so excited about the trip. See you tomorrow," Kim bubbled as she finished zipping her jacket.

167

That night at dinner Dad showed me an article on the dog thieves. They were still in jail. They had made a plea bargain for the dog thefts. "Does it say why they did it?"

Dad pointed to a section which I read out loud, "The pair were arrested for a fight shortly after returning from their last tour of duty in Afghanistan. They were convicted of aggravated assault. While they weren't given prison time they ended up with a criminal record. No one would hire them so they started their own business. They did odd jobs, mostly salvage using leads from the bargain box in the St. Cloud Times. An add for free puppies led them to find markets for dogs. Not finding enough free dogs they stole them."

"That is so sad," Mom sighed. "Does it say why they shot Sara?"

"No, she's not mentioned. The article does say that the two gave them excellent leads on some criminal enterprises still being investigated."

Chapter Seventy

The next day seeing Kim's parents off went as planned. Kim and Marcia settled into my room. I slept on a rollaway bed with Max. The last school days before Christmas vacation were uneventful.

On Christmas Eve after breakfast everyone piled into the Dodge Caravan Peaches had borrowed from her parents. Two huge tins of Christmas cookies fit nicely in the storage area beneath our feet. A hymnal perched on each seat ready for us to sing carols as we drove. I sang joyfully, without chest pain.

When we entered the soup kitchen I greeted the boy in the wheelchair. "Conner, I didn't know you would be here."

"I'm on the welcoming committee every Christmas Eve."

"It's my first time," I confessed.

Everyone had greeted Conner by name as they entered so I wasn't surprised when he said, "Your family has been part of the team as long as I can remember. I see you brought Kim and her sister. Are they in your family too?"

Marcia said, "No, we're her neighbors. We're staying with her while our parents go on a second honeymoon."

Mom approached slipping red aprons on us and directing us to help set out the place mats and silverware. More of the extended family arrived. Soon there were three people for every task. Marcia joined Conner greeting the people. Kim and I helped people carry their plates to the table. When everyone was served all of us volunteers filled our plates and sat in the empty spots around the room. By two o'clock as the crowd thinned we helped with dishes. We were home in time for Peaches and Jerry to return the van and get to their college church to help with the services. After an informal pizza break my friends, parents and I headed for the eight o'clock Christmas Eve services. By ten thirty our tired family sat around the Christmas tree listening to seasonal music from the radio.

Peaches and Jerry returned with an armful of wrapped presents which they passed out. Kim and Marcia were surprised by the gifts they held. Mom passed out the other gifts that were under the tree. Marcia ran upstairs and brought down my special gift.

Peaches commented, "Marcia, did you wrap that?"

"No, my birthfather did," I admitted.

The stunned group looked at me for an explanation.

I blushed. Kim explained, "When we were at Sara's old house We found a bag that had this gift in it from her dad. Sara didn't want to open it until Christmas."

All watched as I carefully unwrapped a polished nine inch wooden cube.

"It's a jewelry box," announced Marcia as she pointed to a tiny dot.

I pushed the dot and the top opened revealing a shimmering deep purple and white necklace. Tears filled my eyes as I put it on.

"There's a note inside," Peaches pointed out. "Do you want me to read it?"

"Please," I muttered quietly.

She read: *"Your handcrafted box in Brazilian pernambuco and purpleheart wood contains a unique necklace of deep amethyst, sea pearls and abalone commissioned for Sara by her father."*

"Thanks, Dad," I said while looking into Max's eyes and then gave him a hug. I composed myself and requested, "Lets get on with opening presents."

Mom beamed thanks for the cake pan then fell silent when she opened it and found her sister's blouse, the one she had secretly coveted.

Besides the gifts left by their parents, Kim and Marcia received some dragonfly necklaces, fancy socks and scarves. They gave me the book, <u>The No. 1 Ladies' Detective Agency</u> by Alexander McCall Smith while Jerry and Peaches gave me the DVD from the PBS series based on the same book.

By midnight we all were asleep in bed. Jerry and Peaches were camped out on the couch.

Chapter Seventy-One

The next morning "Joy to the World" blasted from the stereo at eight o'clock. We were already up and adding the final jeweled touches to our outfits. Mom and Dad prepared breakfast and were surprised at our prompt arrival. Then Jerry and Peaches entered each tethered to a dog.

"We'll take the dogs in our car," Jerry announced.

Mom and Dad looked at each other. They had debated all week about whether to take them. Mitzy had always been welcome. They thought two dogs might be an imposition. Mom ended the debate with, "Thanks, Jerry."

A slow breakfast and cleanup ended in time for us to head to the extended family celebration. The meal would be a repeat of the Thanksgiving dinner except ham and roast beef replaced the turkeys. As people arrived, food went in the refrigerator or in crock pots and ovens to be ready for a two o'clock meal.

The youngest family members were showing off their Christmas toys. Uncle Roger took the wrapped gifts and placed them near each intended recipient. At one o'clock his wife, Aunt Shelly began leading the group in the carols we all knew by heart.

Uncle Roger noted, "The gifts still under the tree have no names on them. Does everyone have a gift?"

"Those are extra," Gina admitted, "in case someone showed up unexpected."

Uncle Roger humorously suggested, "If anyone doesn't like their gift, feel free to exchange it."

We opened our gifts one at a time beginning with the youngest. When Marcia's turn came she opened a fancy box of Kleenex and waited for the next person to open their gift.

Cousin Gary admonished, "Look inside the box."

She pulled out one tissue. Screamed. Jumped up and down in joy. She plucked out a cell phone. She ran to Aunt Linda gratefully hugging her.

Kim looked a little jealous. The gift in her hand definitely was a bottle of bubble bath. As she pulled the paper apart the plastic bottle broke open. A rock fell out. She moved the tissue paper to reveal she too had gotten a phone.

Aunt Pearl explained, "Linda and I were getting new phones. We knew you girls didn't have phones. Your parents okayed our giving you our old phones. We didn't think you would mind white elephants that took selfies."

Peaches, Gina and Aunt Linda were all overwhelmed when each opened their gifts. When Linda complained the brooch was too valuable to accept, I countered with, "Elephants aren't cheap."

Aunt Linda explained, "Sara, this pin was your grandmother's. She wore it often. I told her that someday I wanted a pin like that. She offered to will it to me when she died. Then she died without a will."

"So it's supposed to be yours," I affirmed.

With all the gifts unwrapped and everyone properly thanked, the family moved to the table for dinner. Board games, card games and an outdoor game of frisbee followed. Kim and Marcia felt comfortable blending into various activities, surprised at the mix of ages in each group.

On the ride home all proclaimed it the best Christmas ever.

Chapter Seventy-Two

Christmas vacation flew. On Monday, I woke with the glow from the perfect weekend that began the new year. After greeting my parents and pouring milk on my cereal I let out a sigh of relief. I had enjoyed Kim and Marcia staying with us but felt relieved on Wednesday when their parents came back.

"You seem as content as a kitten with a bowl of cream," noted Dad.

"I am. Good," I paused to think of the right word, "simile, Dad."

"Well, Sara, it looks like you're taking literature seriously," Mom applauded.

"I am. Dad, is there anything about the Philippines in the paper?"

"Is today current affairs day?" Noting my grunt of agreement he continued, "There are several articles. You can take the whole paper if you want."

"No, thanks. I'll just take this first section. You've read it, right?"

"Makes no difference. If our daughter needs the paper, she shall have it."

"Thanks, Dad," I uttered while taking the newspaper and giving him a kiss. I kissed Mom. "I'm off to catch the bus. See you tonight."

"Well, that's new," Dad noted. "You sure are in a great mood. Why?"

"I think the relaxing, fun weekend we had did it, " I suggested while closing the door.

To my delight, Kim had walked down to catch the bus with me. "Kim, how was the weekend catching up on your parents travels?"

"Great we even played games together. Oh no," Kim exclaimed when she saw the newspaper in my hand. "Today's current events and I don't have anything."

"I can share my paper. I'm taking the articles on the super typhoon," I ripped two pages out and a short section of the first page entitled, "Typhoon Death Toll Could Hit 10,000." I handed the remaining sheets to Kim as we boarded the bus.

"Thanks, this article on battlefields to oil field looks interesting."

"Sorry, I've got a part of that article on the back of mine. I'm sure there are other interesting articles."

"Of course, there are others," Kim sprung back amazing herself. As she scanned the remaining paper she called out possibilities: "Minnesota's campaign database isn't adding up," adding, "too complicated."

"Politics is always complicated and boring," I agreed.

"How about this article on cardiac pumps? Oh here's a better one, much shorter about helping people in Myanmar because so many of them are blind."

"Isn't that the country with two names?" I inquired.

"You mean Myanmar, formerly known as Burma? I don't see Burma mentioned in the article, which is good. If I gave both names some smart aleck will ask me why it has two names. I don't know, do you?"

"No, but I need to finish reading this article. We're almost at school and current events is first."

As she folded the rest of the paper into her backpack, Kim sighed with relief, "I have a study hall before current events. See you after school."

Chapter Seventy-Three

After the class settled for first period, Herman Montale was first for current affairs. As expected he took a creepy subject, explaining the use of fecal transplants. When he said he would explain what "fecal" meant Mrs. Wilson cut him short with, "Herman, we all know what it means. Now tell us how this news affects your life."

"My cousin has Crohn's disease and it might help her."

I was next.

"My article is really three on the Super typhoon that hit the Philippines on Friday. I'll pass this one around because it is mostly pictures."

Mrs. Wilson asked, "Andy, you have a question?"

I expected a wise crack about global warming.

Looking at me he quipped, "Doesn't God send those storms because the people were witch doctors or doing bad things?"

Tired of his harassment I had been rehearsing a comeback. With determination I shot back, "No, absolutely not? What kind of God do you believe in that would want to wipe out 10,000 people, including kids and babies?" I was on a roll. I remembered and shared my birthfather's words, "My God is not a knit-picking bean counter, treating us like a video game." Aunt Pearl's wisdom surfaced. "If you think everything happens for a reason, you are a puppet with no choices. God pulls you here and there and kills you whenever. I don't believe that. My God is love."

Feeling Joan of Arc confident I loudly demanded, "I am tired of you making the comment when I am around that my parents died because they were sinful and didn't go to church every Sunday. Who do you think you are judging my parents? An accident is an accident. A girl was dumb enough to be texting while driving. Her choices took away our choices. God cries with me over the tragedy. My parents are in heaven. I am choosing to make good come out of their death."

I took a breath. The principal had slipped in. I didn't care. I spoke a little softer but with as much determination, "Am I clear Andy Parta?" I didn't give him time to answer. "I chose this article because my Cousin Gina's family lives in the Philippines. Her husband helped them reenforce their house when they visited last year. Their house is the only one standing in that area so her parents are sheltering their neighbors. They haven't heard from Gina's father's family who are in the area of the most destruction. God loves them and expects us to pray for them and help them."

I had never felt so angry and motivated as I was then. I ran out of the room grabbing the hall pass to make it legal. I began crying and didn't see the principal approach. Then I felt her arms embracing me, holding me up. "Let's go to the office."

Keeping her arm around me she escorted me past the principal's office into the psychologist's office, empty because of budget cuts. She eased me into a chair, handing me a box of tissues, giving me all the time I needed to cry.

The crying subsided. As I stood to leave I apologized, "Sorry."

"You have nothing to apologize for. You have been through a lot. I apologize that we hadn't stopped Andy from bullying you. If it ever happens again order him to the principal's office and then tell any teacher that you were bullied. Understand?"

I nodded.

177

"You're staying here for first period." She activated some ice packs, giving them to me to put on my eyes. I laid down on the couch for twenty minutes until the swelling went down. Then I got up and went back to class grateful no one in the office stopped me.

I passed Andy in the hall. My fiery eyes drove the smugness from his. He shuffled his way to the principal's office. That was the last any of us saw of Andy Parta.

Chapter Seventy-Four

I entered the classroom as everyone stood to leave. High-fives, fist bumps and words of praise were lavished on me as I gathered my things and throughout the morning.

At lunch I felt something on my head. I took off the paper crown Isad had placed on my head which boldly proclaimed me as "Sara, the Bully Slayer."

Isad stood behind me giggling. I turned around and quizzed her, "How did you find out?"

"Good news travels fast." Isad winked and left.

The usual Kimsara crew gathered for lunch, complimenting me on putting Andy in his place. I blushed and tried to focus everyone on plans for Friday.

RT updated everyone. "The sheriff will be here on Friday for a school assembly. Kimsara will be recognized for its help in catching the dog thieves."

I reminded everyone, "The Kimsara Detective Agency isn't just Kim and me."

"Right," Abdi agreed. "Peter, Conner and I have put together a little skit explaining the expanded meaning of Kimsara, like it's on our website."

"Sara, you wanted all of us in any pictures the newspaper wants to take," Emma reminded me. "Doesn't that put all of us in danger? I mean, you got shot. Is it safe for us to be in the paper?

"Good point," commented Kim.

"We could have the paper not to print our names, couldn't we?" suggested Peter.

"I'll check on that," I offered.

"We could also wear disguises," RT suggested to a chorus of groans. "Hear me out. We have those glasses with fake noses from the Halloween party."

"How many do you have?" asked Abdi.

"More than enough," admitted RT "They came in a pack of 48. I'll bring them, we can decide on Friday if we want to use them."

After lunch I stopped in the principal's office. "Principal Jones," I said. "On Friday the police are coming to thank the Kimsara Detective Agency. In case some of the media come out for it and take pictures, is it possible to tell them they can't print our names? I don't want anyone put in danger for being associated with us."

"I understand, Sara. That shouldn't be a problem. Have your ribs healed?"

"Pretty much so. You know that some from Kimsara are planning on a short presentation to invite more kids to get involved in keeping each other safe."

"Yes, Conner and Peter ran the program by me. I didn't realize so many from the school were involved."

"Along with our school we have a third grader and some students in Hopkins involved. Got to get to class. Thanks for your help, Principal Jones," I called back as I left the office.

Chapter Seventy-Five

That evening when I got home from school, I walked the dogs. I was working on my homework on the kitchen table when my mom exited her office to check on supper. Five minutes later my father entered commenting, "Sorry, you had such a rough day, Sara."

At first I didn't understand what he meant.

"Art, how do you know about Sara's day?" questioned Mom as I checked the dinner cooking in the crock pot.

"Joe Parta called me at work to apologize for what his son, Andy, had done to you," Dad explained.

Cautiously I asked, "What did he say Andy did?"

"It almost made sense. Guess Andy said God sent the typhoon to the Philippines to kill the people who weren't doing God's will. Also, he's been saying your parents are in hell."

"Then I yelled at him and walked out of the room," I confessed.

"Andy's father pulled him from school to get his son straightened out," Dad reported.

"Does that mean he's sending him to military school?" considered Mom.

"He didn't say."

"I feel sorry for Andy," I admitted. "He is so sure he knows exactly what God is thinking, but then describes such a cruel God."

Together we got dinner on the table and the dogs fed. As dinner wound down, I remembered, "You're invited to the school assembly, last period on Friday. The police are coming out to publicly thank the Kimsara Detective Agency. The thieves pled guilty and are behind bars."

Both Dad and Mom said they would try to make it.

On Friday morning I debated on wearing my best dress or jeans to school. I chose jeans and my best plush sweater in undulating shades of azure and ultramarine. With guaranteed police presence, my father's necklace would get its inaugural viewing. Thus the orange butterfly blouse would miss this stellar occasion.

Once I took my jacket off, everyone commented on my necklace. I became uneasy with the attention so tucked it under my sweater.

At lunch the Kimsara Detective Agency modeled the best from each member's closet. Abdi's crisp white shirt contrasted his rich ebony face. Kim's elegant hand-me-down dress from me floated around her. Several teased Peter for appearing without his usual t-shirt advertising his family's Mexican restaurant.

RT, looking more professional than usual, cracked everyone up when he put on Groucho glasses. He questioned, "Well, do we want to wear these?"

Above the grumbling Peter countered, "Isn't the question, do we **need** to wear them? Kimsara's exists to stop our dogs being stolen. We did that."

Emma continued, "We're kids. What other mysteries will we ever solve?"

"I'd like to know what happened to Andy Parta," Abdi mused. "Emma's probably right today is our swan song. We're done."

"Swan song?" several blurted out.

"Look it up," challenged Abdi.

"The end of Kimsara," Kim lamented.

"I doubt it," I prophesied. "Lunch, however, is definitely over. See everyone at assembly."

Chapter Seventy-Six

As students gathered for the last period assembly Kim and I waved all those connected with Kimsara to the stage. A few like Isad were surprised at the invitation. The ramp had been set out so Conner could join us. Two television stations and a number of reporters with cameras milled around.

Some officers from the Hopkins police department had set up a camera. On the big screen TV another assembly appeared. Officer Lee wheeled in with the county sheriff, followed by several from the Whistlestop Police Department.

The principal addressed the assembly. "Welcome everyone to this joint news conference conducted by the Whistlestop and Sherburne County police in tandem with the Hopkins police. On the TV screen we can see the Hopkins assembly. Hopkins, can you hear us?"

The loud response indicated they could. She turned the microphone over to the county sheriff, Tim Nixon, who announced, "We are here because the Kimsara Detective Agency operating from this school has been instrumental in solving several cases. Before we honor them, they've prepared a little skit to tell you what the agency is." He sat down.

Conner wheeled to the front of the stage. Adjusting the microphone he began, "A year and a half ago my assistance dog, Rex, was stolen. Everyone said he ran away. We called the police but they couldn't help. Other kids' dogs went missing. Finally on the bus one day two students formed a detective agency to find our dogs. We knew it was too late for most of us to get our dogs back but we could stop other dogs from being stolen. From two people the Agency has grown so now Kimsara stands for many things including..."

The microphone circulated from student to student with each one giving a different interpretation of Kimsara. Kim ended with: "Kids In Modern Schools: Aware, Responsible, Active. Many from the Kimsara Detective Agency are here on stage. In addition our parents, neighbors, brothers and sisters have been part of our success. We would like to invite everyone here to become active in observing what is happening around them so we can stop trouble before it becomes serious."

Then I spoke, "We'd like to thank Billy and the kids in Hopkins who helped out. They supplied the picture that identified the thieves. We're happy they could join us today."

I handed the microphone back to the sheriff. As I sat down I slipped my necklace back on top of my sweater.

The sheriff stood and said, "Today we publicly thank the Kimsara Detective Agency for service above and beyond the call of duty. I award this plaque which will be put in the school trophy case. Could the Kimsara Detective Agency please stand for a picture?" As planned, Conner accepted the plaque for the group. We gathered around him for the picture while everyone in the auditorium clapped. Cameras flashed.

"Thank you, Sheriff Nixon," a voice spoke from the TV screen. "Likewise, the Hopkins Police Department would like to give Billy Austin and his friends a commendation for their role in helping apprehend the thieves." A group of twelve stood up to receive the award.

184

The Sherburne County Sheriff again spoke. "I want to publicly acknowledge what the students at these two schools have done.

"The loss of a few pets doesn't seem like a major crime wave. After searching the premises of the thieves we found documents chronicling the sale of the dogs. This allowed us to close down and prosecute people running two dog fighting rings.

"Some dogs were sold to a fraudulent assistant dog program which charged customers thousands of dollars for dogs who were not adequately trained. That program has been shut down. A task force is trying to contact the buyers to see if seized assets can be used to pay for the retraining or replacement of their dogs.

"Many dogs went to unlicensed labs which conducted product safety tests. Some were sold to pet stores, two of which have been closed for knowingly buying stolen property.

"All of this was possible because a few students believed their dogs weren't running away but were being stolen. They put together compelling evidence which they passed on to our IT Officer, Lee Petersen. Officer Lee, would you please come forward."

Officer Lee rolled up the platform onto the stage. The mayor of Whistlestop approached the microphone. He said, "Officer Lee on behalf of the citizens of Whistlestop," he paused pointing to the TV screen where the mayor of Hopkins could be seen.

He continued, "And the Citizens of Hopkins present this Distinguished Service Award for listening to our children and helping them stop so much crime." Everyone clapped.

Officer Lee took the microphone saying, "Thank you. It's hard not to listen when the kids make such well documented and compelling arguments. I'd like to thank everyone in the department who took their findings seriously and helped in the investigations."

185

Chapter Seventy-Seven

Officer Lee spoke into her radio then continued to address the group. "We have records of the group brokering cats and dogs over a three year period. That means a lot of lost pets. Several recently stolen dogs were found. These have been in foster homes to make sure they would make safe pets if returned to their known owners. We contacted parents to verify they wanted them back. Some of the families agreed to meet us here. So I present you with some of the dogs rescued by the Kimsara Detective Agency."

A dozen dogs were led in on leashes.

Ben shot out of his seat screaming, "Mischief." A St. Bernard lunged forward ignoring the leash which quickly dropped as boy and dog united.

My eyes watered as I saw joy in Justin's whole being as he ran to be united with Turbo. I thought Emma cried because she realized her lab was really gone as next to her Matt's miniature cocker spaniel wiggled in his lap. A TV camera had moved in close to capture Matt's joy and was rewarded as a lab dragged a volunteer to Emma's side. Emma had her hands covering her eyes until the lab knocked them away and licked her tears. Emma's ecstasy opened that evening's news.